The Painter of Birds

ALSO BY LÍDIA JORGE

The Murmuring Coast

The Painter of Birds

Lídia Jorge

Translated from the Portuguese
by Margaret Jull Costa

Harcourt, Inc.
NEW YORK   SAN DIEGO   LONDON

This is a translation of *O Vale da Paixão*

www.harcourt.com

This book was supported by the Portuguese Institute for Books and Libraries.

Library of Congress Cataloging-in-Publication Data
Jorge, Lídia.
[Vale da paixao. English]
The painter of birds/Lídia Jorge;
translated from the Portuguese by Margaret Jull Costa.—1st U.S. ed.
p.   cm.
ISBN 0-15-100658-X
I. Costa, Margaret Jull.   II. Title.
PQ9272.O69 V2513 2001
869.3'42—dc21   00-053545

Text set in Centaur MT
First U.S. edition
A C E G I K J H F D B
Printed in the United States of America

For David

Walter Dias' footsteps again pause on the landing, as they did on that night when he visited his daughter; he slips off his shoes and prepares to continue up the stairs, lithe as a shadow and keeping close to the wall, and I cannot dissuade or stop him, for the simple reason that I want him to reach the last step quickly, to open the door without knocking and to cross the narrow threshold without saying a word. And so it was on that first night, before the time for reconstructing all these gestures had passed: there he was in the middle of the room, holding his shoes in one hand. On that far-off winter night, the rain was falling over the sandy plain, and the noise of the rain on the roof tiles protected us from the world and from the others in the house like a drawn curtain that no human force could wrench open. Had it been otherwise, Walter would not have come up the stairs or entered the room.

At that time, the house in Valmares had already lost most of its inhabitants, and the rooms that lined the corridor where everyone used to pass each other, the rooms in which the descendants of Francisco Dias had once lived, were all closed up. Once it had been difficult to distinguish people by their footsteps. The various children and grandchildren, the three daughters-in-law and the son-in-law, all of them up and about from dawn onward, created a multiplicity of sounds that defied all attempts at disentanglement by the child who spent hours on end in her room listening. However, that winter, in the early 1960s, the footsteps of those who had remained were as easily identifiable as their faces or their photos.

There were the light, loose steps of Maria Ema's children, still childlike and uncertain, reminiscent of scampering rodents as they raced up and down the corridor in one fleet flock. In contrast, there were the heavy footsteps of Francisco Dias, which, thanks to the two gleaming lines of tacks on the soles of his boots, had a metallic ring to them that followed him everywhere as if he were wearing a crown on his feet. And then there was Custódio, whose steps were lighter than his father's, but he too wore protective metal tips that occasionally clinked on the tiles or the concrete floor with the asymmetrical gait of the lame. The footsteps of Francisco Dias' eldest son were unmistakable for other reasons too. The syncopated rhythm emerged from the west room that he shared with Maria Ema, and the sound sprang from Custódio's boots like a mistake, an imbalance, like a mismatch between the ground and reality, and yet the regular asymmetry of those footsteps was somehow more regular than all the other footsteps in the Valmares house. She listened for that fault, for the silent foot, like a pendulum that swings and seems about to miss a beat, but never does. There was no mistaking his footsteps, constantly crossing with those of Maria Ema, which, however, never stopped next to his.

2.

For there were her footsteps too, the steps of Maria Ema, Custódio's wife, normally rubber-soled in the morning and leather-soled in the evening, except that now her brother-in-law had come back, she wore high heels all the time. You could hear her around the house, clicking across the tiles, catching on the mats and click-clacking across the wooden floors. You could imagine her walking about in an ankle-length dress, imagine her white legs and slender waist. Those were her footsteps in the large house in Valmares, a house just far enough from the Atlantic not to hear the waves breaking during the storms, but near enough for the walls of the house to be corroded by the saltpeter in the spray. Those were her footsteps, different from the others. But Walter's footsteps were different too.

Walter Dias had returned a month before, wearing fine shoes made from buffalo hide. The softness of the material reduced the impact on the floor, but there was still a faint squeak that came from Walter's feet pressing down on the foam insole as he walked along the empty corridor. Everyone knew those silent, telltale footsteps, soft as a breath and audible as a sigh. As soon as he came in through the front door, Maria Ema's children would shout—"He's here!" Everyone knew when he came in and when he went out. On that night, then, it was just as well that the owner of those foam footsteps should pause cautiously on the landing. Walter Dias came in without knocking and leaned back against the door as soon as he had closed it, covering his own mouth with his hand. "Please, don't call out"—he said on the night when he went up to see his daughter;

3

she was expecting him, though she had never believed he would actually come. And only then did he sit down on a chair, put on his shoes, pick up the lamp, turn the knob until the flame burned green, and then hold up to his own face that flame the shape of a poppy petal. He held it up as if the heart of the flame were a magnifying glass and he stood there looking at her, observing her from the front and the side while the heavy rain did battle with the windows.

3.

Yes, that night, as he held the lamp level with her head, the tall, tremulous flame there before her eyes, and the smell of burning oil pervading the room, the rain came and went, drenching the hot, parched earth, close relative of the desert, and then, in a break in the rain, she suddenly heard the unmistakable footsteps of Custódio Dias. His limping steps. They emerged from the farthest, most westerly part of the house, advanced along the passageway of high doors, crossed the transept where four of those doors met, and then stopped by the landing, where Custódio called out–"Is anyone up there?"

The lamp was turned down, the flame was a glowworm trapped behind the glass, and Walter was protecting it with his hands as he held his breath, standing absolutely still, his knees flexed, as if ready to attack or to defend himself, and she, who had not yet moved from the place where he had found her, wanted to do something to stop those steps, racking her brains for an idea or an action that could avert the danger. Besides, she was convinced that Walter had not come up to her room of his own volition; she had summoned him with her thoughts, and that was why, if Custódio found him hiding in her room, she would be the person responsible for whatever grave thing happened next, just at a time when the house in Valmares was filled, as never before, by fervent joy. Custódio did, in fact, begin to climb the stairs, directing his flashlight up at the door, for the beam of light slipped through the crack underneath and spread across the floor of the room, but Francisco Dias' oldest son stopped halfway and called out again— "Is anyone up there?" Then there was a long, long silence, until he turned on the stairs and went back down. Custódio Dias' unmistakable footsteps went down the stairs, disappeared along the corridor and died away in the west room which, in the 1960s, he shared with Maria Ema. And the rain began pounding down again.

Only then did Walter grip her wrist and lead her to the mirror, open the wardrobe, and then, just as if he had never actually been there, he, in turn, vanished down the dark corridor.

4.

But tonight there is no need for him to cup his hands around a flame, no need to hold his breath. If he did, it would be pure reflex or in memory of a no longer justifiable secrecy. Now Walter Dias can leave the door open and stride across the room in leather-soled shoes or even metal-tipped ones if he cares to, because no one is interested now in our relationship and in our lives. We are protected by the web of forgetting woven by the years and by the harmony that has descended upon the marriage of Maria Ema and Custódio, who are now the house's sole residents.

On summer nights, as if the moon or the stars were masks worn by cynical creatures laughing far off in the distance, husband and wife gaze up ecstatically at the bright heavens, weaving conspiratorially respectful silences. They can do that now because all the awkward objects and awkward people have been packed away in their boxes and there is no one now to punish, no one to kill. They know this, their lives have been beaten to a stiff, perfect peak. Sometimes the olive trees glow white as if their leaves were being sprinkled with silver dust, and they both remark on it as they sit in the deck chairs brought by their children on one of their lightning visits. They also brought them a set of beach umbrellas, which husband and wife never close and beneath whose shade they sit, even at night.

The house, however, remains as it always was. Maria Ema's children agree on that, for they do not have the walls rebuilt, they simply slap on another layer of paint; and Maria Ema and Custódio, hand in hand now, form part of the walls around which their children have drawn up a renovation plan. The idea is to have the façade and the courtyard refurbished and painted and to get in a bulldozer to dig out a blue swimming pool in the shape of a human footprint in the place where Francisco Dias used to keep the manure. The gray fig trees may be cut down and replaced by fully grown palm trees from which white hammocks will be slung. It will also be necessary to remove any trace of the old farm animals from the flagstones and to make the courtyard a pleasant place to walk in. Inside the house, though, the beams will remain, as will the banister, the stairs, the door of the room on the first floor, the handle, the threshold and the wooden floor. Perhaps the same light will remain too and the same sound of footsteps on the floorboards, the same smell of soap and wax. The same landing and the same stairs. That way, whenever he chooses, Walter Dias will be able to walk through the darkness, or even with his eyes closed, and he won't get lost. As she had on that night of footsteps and rain, she would still want Walter Dias to come up to his daughter's room, smiling as usual, and to do so purely in order to visit her.

Because there was a moment on that night in 1963 when Walter Dias stood stock-still in the middle of the room and, holding up the oil lamp with its tremulous flame, said—"I chose India rather than you, but you were worth more than India, and more than the journey there and back too. Do you understand?" And she was so surprised, so overcome by confusion, that she couldn't speak or think. It seemed impossible to her that Walter Dias should have come all that way and crept into her room carrying his shoes in his hand, like a burglar, merely to beg her forgiveness for something which she clutched to herself like a gift. "You were worth more than India," he was saying at that moment, as if he felt no joy to be there in the room.

5.

This was before Custódio Dias' footsteps had come halfway up the stairs, and the flame in the lamp was still burning high.

The rain came and went like a curtain that was one moment drawn shut and the next ripped asunder, and he added, still holding up the lamp and with his eyes fixed on hers—"I've never given you anything." And she was utterly astonished, for she knew it wasn't true, and she wanted to prove to him that it wasn't, that she was surrounded by the objects and the people he had left behind, by images, ideas, reasons, clothes and drawings all belonging to him, and that the only reason she had yearned for this meeting was simply to explain to him how she lived with him, in his absence, through all the things of his that she possessed. She wanted to tell him he owed her nothing, on the contrary, that everything was as perfect as a correctly calculated multiplication sum, which will stand until the end of logic and the end of time. But no explanation was possible that night, perhaps because she did not have the right words or, if she did, could not put them in the right order; at least that is what happened in the surprising moment of his visit. She felt profoundly shocked by his declaration, and it seemed strange to her that he should run such a risk simply in order to hold a lamp to her face and tell her how he had wronged her. How absurd to say he had never given her anything.

She managed to think that, but she could not say it.

And when Custódio's footsteps had died away, Walter turned up the flame again and began to make promises about the fortune he wanted to prepare for her, a marvelous legacy that would consist in part of airports and wide roads, of universities with Doric columns and Greek inscriptions, a world of dollars, business deals and journeys. If, one day, they should make a trip to the Panama Canal, he would show her his favorite birds and the sound of them singing all at once. He liked the birds in hot countries, but when it came to living and making money, he preferred colder countries. For some reason, he had started out in India, but now was based in a land of snow. Initially, he would, in fact, be taking her to a cold place, and later they would make occasional trips south, but he would not rest easy until he had taken his daughter to view the Statue of Liberty from the Hudson River. She would go there with him, God willing. And, God willing, he was in a position to offer her a free country, free trade and free love. "I'll pay you back everything I owe you, you'll see"–said Walter Dias on that winter night in 1963, when the oil in the lamp was beginning to burn down.

She remembers that part of the night and the passionate way he spoke to her–"Can you imagine, a Turkish man burst into tears on the deck of the ship when he first saw the Statue of Liberty. I did too. And you'll feel exactly the same as that Turk." And at that point it became clear that the oil would not last until dawn. Indeed, how could it, when it was obvious there would only be that one night? Yes, we only had one night, that night of rain, and knowing we were living through that night with no possibility of ever repeating it prevented us from really experiencing it. But tonight feels so close to that other night they seem like one, locked between sunset and sunrise. Who cares about the long day that lay in between?

6.

Just as he did then, Walter arrives with his shoes in his hand, wearing his light-colored raincoat over his dark suit, and he comes in, but he doesn't shut the door, he doesn't put his shoes on, he doesn't light a lamp, he doesn't sit down or get up. He remains motionless at the door, as if intimidated, which is wrong, because he has come to ask forgiveness when there is absolutely no need for any self-justification. No need at all. The object he sent through the post from Corrientes de Arena was all she could have wanted, an addition to the work of chance. There is no need to repeat himself or to stand there motionless. Walter Dias has come to reiterate the words he himself wrote in his unmistakable forward-slanting hand—*I leave to my niece, as sole inheritance, this soldier's blanket.* And in the top right-hand corner of the visiting card is a small drawing of a bird.

No, not a drawing, a sketch, a seal, a kind of mark, the basic outline of a bird. A sketch of a migratory bird, perhaps a cross between a stilt and an Arctic tern. Perhaps it was a bird that has never existed. The card was tucked into the folds of the blanket. For what he had sent her was his old army blanket, two square meters of rough cloth, the edges bound in brown. None of this would have any importance if it had not been sent by him and if the blanket had not been perfectly clean and so well preserved that, in one corner, you could still see the insignia of the Sixteenth Infantry Regiment. The blanket belonged, it says, to Recruit 687 of '45, car driver, name: Walter Glória Dias, known for his whistle, his walk and for the creatures he used to draw, known too as soldier Walter. She received it this very morning and spread it out on the floor of this room. But, as I said, on the card itself he wrote the message with great care, with the same secretive care that made him take off his shoes to go up to the room in which his daughter lay sleeping.

Besides, on that night, although there was no sign of the blanket, it was there nonetheless. Once Custódio Dias' footsteps had disappeared and the flame had grown tall again and the rain was falling softly, he himself said—"I dread to think what they've told you about me!" He laughed, he was always laughing. "I bet they told you I was a wastrel, a soldier, and about a blanket I used to lie down on when I went off drawing birds. I dread to think what they told you about that blanket and those birds... They probably described me as a con man, a globe-trotter and an adventurer. I bet they poisoned your mind against me. What did they tell you?" For a moment his face drained of joy, and he was seized by a kind of all-consuming anger that made his eyes grow pale. "Tell me what they told you. Tell me the truth..."

But she didn't know what they had said, because she had always transformed everything she had heard, and that was why she could not explain to Walter Dias, however insistent he was and however much she wanted to respond to his insistence, because she had never thought about the discrepancy between what she had been told and what she had heard. And even if she had been able to summarize what she knew, which was very little, there was no time, because the oil was running out and the glass was growing dark. All she could say was that she associated only good things with him, and that, on that brief night visit, there was no time to tell him about all the good things she had saved up; being mere words they would not fit into that moment watched over by the powerful hand of the rain. It wasn't really worth beginning. With Walter there so near, why waste time saying, for example, that she had always known Maria Ema had been the wife of two men, and that Francisco Dias was her grandfather twice over? That she had always been aware of an ambiguity, a duplication, the resultant of a double entity that had become fused into one at some point in the prehistory of its lives?

She was perfectly aware that her three brothers, the children of Maria Ema and Custódio Dias, were not her true brothers. She knew her brothers were also her cousins, that the same blood that united them also separated them. And she knew that all her identification papers contained a lie, but she colluded with that lie, because out of the ambiguity emerged events so warm and fertile they might have been born out of truths, as if fertility and joy sprang up not along the straight banks of the true and the false, but in very different soil. She recalled wonderful, unforgettable moments that were all related to concealment and lying, such as when Fernandes, Adelina Dias' husband, first taught her the letter W.

She didn't remember him, only his apprentice electrician's hand and his voice at her shoulder saying—"Make two Vs joined at the bottom, right on the line, that's it." Fernandes' low voice and Fernandes' agile hand writing the W. "And now in your own hand write Walter Glória Dias." And he himself had written the letter on a sheet of white paper. And that had been a good day, a hot afternoon, when the children had been put in charge of driving the flocks of chickens out of the yard with long canes. And not even the fact that the chickens had invaded the flower beds that very afternoon and dug up the flowers, scattering manure everywhere, not even that unfortunate fact had diminished the joy of drawing those two Vs which looked like an M floating head downward, or two Vs flying with their wings erect. Walter's daughter had acquired a twenty-fourth letter to add to the normal twenty-three of the Portuguese alphabet, but she was not to speak of it because Fernandes' voice would not let her. "Write a W, W for Walter and for Watt too, we learn about that in Electricity," he was saying, though he did not belong in the Valmares house. He left with the first wave of recruits, leaving that secret letter with her forever.

And had there been time, had she had a substantial part of the night at her disposal, she could have explained all that and could even have acquitted herself quite well, once she had summarized a whole string of tales and fables, beginning perhaps with a few lines from *The Iliad—Leave, go, pernicious dream, to the fine ships of the Achaeans. When you are in the tent of the Atreid Agamemnon, speak exactly as I have taught you, without omitting a single detail, leave.* She would have liked to say it out loud so that Walter Dias could hear. But since she could not recite or summarize what she could not recite because of the time trickling away, he had to repeat several times, without obtaining a reply—"Tell me what they told you, tell me what you know about us!" And then, holding the lamp at shoulder height, he said—"There are so many things I never gave you!" Said Walter Dias, in his pale raincoat, drenched on the shoulders and down the front, proof that he could not stay there, that we had no time.

7.

But an hour or only a matter of minutes before, Walter had started making promises in a voice so low most of his words were lost, not that it mattered. The promises Walter made that night were unforgettable because, although the sheer weight of rainwater on the roof tiles made his words barely intelligible, it also gave them a musical beat, while the promises in Walter's eyes and on his lips were creating images of color and speed. And yet, there was no need for him to have said, "God, there are so many things I never gave you!" And he kept promising and promising. And as I said, she heard the words but not the promises, because she wasn't interested in what he was promising. It didn't interest her that he should be saying what he was saying, as if, concealed beneath his raincoat, in the middle of his chest, there was a box that kept emitting those strange words, "I owe you so much!"

And just to console him, she would have liked to drag herself away from the headboard she was leaning against and to go over to the drawer in the table where she kept all his sketches and just leaf through them, so that he could see with his own eyes how much he had given her without ever having to make any promises. For how could Walter Dias owe her anything when she had in her room Walter Dias' *Album of Birds,* which had grown under her watchful eye as sole owner of all his work? Walter did not know the route they had taken. He used to send them to his brother Custódio as if they were intended for him when, in fact, they were for Maria Ema, and when Maria Ema had gone through them and discarded each one, the drawings passed to Walter's daughter. The album grew slowly, irregularly, patiently, the way a tree grows, the way the slow, long-awaited fruit grow and ripen. And that is what she should have told Walter that night and thus stopped his lips from making all those promises. She would have preferred his lips to be still, quiet, sealed, so that she could gaze on their silence, dumb as the drenched surface of his raincoat, just as she had imagined she would before she had made him come up to her room. But she couldn't.

She wanted to tell him that in Valmares the postman arrived on a bicycle and that, from time to time, he would deliver a letter from Walter to his eldest brother, and that, seated at the table made out of chestnut wood, his father Francisco Dias would declare—"Ah, a letter from the wanderer! Read it to us." Occasionally, one of the other brothers would listen to the beginning, but there were so many of them around the table, each one intent on his own business or his own food, that no one listened properly. Custódio only read it for his father, who would repeat any sentences that merited his mockery or his rage. Only after Custódio had read it out loud did he pass it to his wife along with the drawing of a bird that accompanied each letter.

Yes, I was a witness to the fact that Maria Ema used to read the letters by the window, study the drawings, keep them for a while, then pass them back later to the official addressee, who would then pile them up next to the other letters on the bureau in the corridor. Gradually, the pile of drawings became a sheaf of loose leaves in a cover which the brothers would refer to as *Her Album of Birds.* She would stand by the bureau studying the drawings. The cuckoo from India, the ibis from Mozambique, the hummingbird from the West Indies or the goose from Labrador were there for everyone to see, even though they were hers alone. It was a right won by custom, for without anyone's ever actually saying so, that album which everyone could leaf through was hers. Even if everyone else touched them, she felt herself to be the true inheritor of Walter's drawings. She waited for them, regarded them at a distance, leafed through them when the others weren't there, copied them, removed them to safe places, only to replace them later in their rightful position, discreetly, so that no one would see. Replacing them in the cover, sheet upon sheet, until the album became such a familiar object that their being collected together seemed the natural fate for those drawings of birds. The person who used to send them was Walter, and on that rainy night, she had them there within reach. How then could he say over and over that he had never given her anything?

That is why, if the gutters had not been rotten and the

slates crooked, and if the mournful rain had not kept falling, now calmly, now furiously, she would have opened the desk drawer and shown him the care she took of those birds, so that he would understand why she was so surprised by the endless promises she could read on his lips. What promises were needed on that night when she had brought him to her by sheer force of thought, and he had obeyed and appeared in her room carrying his shoes in his hand? "Please, don't speak. Don't move. Just listen!" he had said.

No, he didn't need to ask for her forgiveness, that wasn't why she had called him. She had so much, she had everything she could possibly want. If that night were to be repeated, she would tell him how she remembered his return from India, and the way in which she had preserved that return, a film of far more importance than *The Blue Angel* or *Anna Karenina*, far more important than any of the other films she had seen—the film of Walter Dias. She would have liked to tell him that she was fifteen, but that she could watch Walter's film whenever she wanted, wherever she was, and that he always appeared, just as he was now, and just as he was then, and that the film was an intangible inheritance, invisible to the others, but real to her, a film in which no one came or left unless she chose. A film about Walter's return.

She would have liked to explain how she had inherited his return to Valmares, when the house was still home to the brigade of cultivators of the soil who had subsequently fled. When the house was still occupied by the Dias brothers— blurred, silent, tense figures, whom she imagined jumping onto wooden carts or sitting around the table—and certain corners of the house were filled for her by the presence of Walter. She had been left with the image of his figure pacing the tiled floors, from the front, from behind, by the table, sitting among the others, and, later, alone, in the buggy. She had inherited that movement, back and forth, standing, walking, with no actual narrative, but repeated and persistent nevertheless. She had all that recorded on film on the night when Walter came up the stairs to the room in the dark and held up the lamp and approached his daughter. "Don't call out!" he had said at first. "Don't move."

8.

No, she wouldn't move, she would stay leaning against the headboard, and yet she would have liked to thank him for coming in through the broad front door in 1951, into the house of his brothers, his sister and sisters-in-law, the house where Maria Ema and the small daughter whom Walter called his niece were living, and he, dressed in khaki, with his white teeth and long, curly hair and his skin burned by the Goan sun and by the journey, as one might expect in a man on leave from the army, coming in through the door of his father's house.

The soldier had become a quartermaster and, after rounding the Cape and having seen half the world, had come home. The dogs leapt up at him. The family were expecting him, but they did not react like the dogs. At the far end of the table sat Maria Ema, married to Custódio Dias, and his daughter was probably also around somewhere. It was the time of great hope for Francisco Dias, the busiest time for a rural community. They were eating a hasty lunch, and, despite the dogs' joy, it was clear that Walter Dias played no part in the family enterprise, created as it was in the likeness of a hard, oppressive state. Even Walter Dias must have realized he had been wrong to come back. He didn't belong there anymore. His brothers knew nothing of the seabirds he spoke about, involved as they were in arduous tasks in the fields. Francisco Dias' lands were turning his sons into harsh, reserved people, as calloused as the palms of their hands. Before Walter had even opened his trunk, he knew he was in the way, that everyone wanted him to leave again. But there was no point in rushing or getting out the knives. Walter would leave when he chose to. You could see it in his face. And it was for the image of that face, growing larger and eclipsing all others, that she wanted to thank him, but could not.

In 1951, Walter was dressed from head to toe in khaki, walking about the house in Valmares like someone exploring the jungle, and he showed them the equipment which the commandant of the Sixteenth Infantry Regiment had given him three years before for certain services rendered. The brothers' plates were pushed to one side, and on the table, along with the boots, scarf, uniform and cap that belonged to him by law, Walter placed a greatcoat and a wide belt which he should have handed back, and even a revolver. A Smith revolver that the commandant had given him for his personal protection. He spun it around on one finger and put it down on the table, laughing. But none of this would have been of any importance if Walter had asked his sister Adelina or even Alexandrina to find a special place in the house in which to keep his kit. Instead he asked his sister-in-law. "Find a good place, a special place, all right?"–he had said to Maria Ema. All the brothers were sitting stiffly around the table, as gravely as if they were at supper with Christ, except that there was no Christ, only the traitor. And Adelina Dias cried out–"Pa, come in here! Walter's flirting with Maria Ema, in front of everyone!" At least that is what happens in that 1951 film.

Then his brothers and his sister, with the exception of Custódio, Maria Ema and the little girl, asked Walter if he had enough money to leave Valmares. If he didn't, that could prove highly problematic. But the intelligence of Francisco Dias' children was rolled up tight inside their skulls and would occasionally reveal itself in all its splendid density. For their reasoning was both complex and dense: "If we have to make a sacrifice in order to have some peace, then that's what we'll have to do." Yes, they were prepared to make a great sacrifice. Each brother would scrape together a thousand escudos from the money saved in their trouser pockets, which, multiplied by seven, would be enough to convey their youngest brother to the ends of the earth. They made the calculations in their heads, drawing on only a tiny corner of their intelligence. Yes, it was agreed.

But the memory did not stop there—Walter had placed his right hand on the pocket of his yellow jacket, he had patted the pocket, stroked it, then drawn from it a bundle of notes, which he had displayed, counting out the notes one by one among the plates, piling them up in the middle of the table, saying he didn't need their money or their hunting dogs, that he had come home only in order to deposit his uniform there, because his one desire was to leave again. He was laughing, always laughing. What did his brothers know about life? In Australia, a good truck driver who didn't mind taking his chances on desert roads and who knew how to drive a Land Rover could make more money in a single year than they would in a whole lifetime of digging the narrow fields of Valmares. And he didn't even need to go driving into the outback, he knew how to earn money on the coast. Besides, when you traveled, you got to see all kinds of different birds, he said. "Birds? Pa, he's saying he earned all that money painting birds!"—Adelina had screamed. "Did you really earn that money with birds?" asked one of the brothers, it doesn't matter which. Because they were all sitting around the table, laughing. Those young, hard Dias faces were laughing a proper rural laugh, they laughed until they cried. Yes, they laughed. It is a late spring day in Valmares, an image cut out of the unvarying heat—him, the table, the pile of notes, his brothers and sisters helpless with laughter around the table. And on the table, still intact, the objects that would become part of the daughter's material inheritance. In that year of 1951, Walter had his army blanket rolled up under his left arm. Adelina screamed out again—"Pa, he hasn't changed, he's got his blanket under his arm!"

Then Walter wandered through the overcrowded house. No one could understand how a quartermaster and a painter of birds could possibly have made all that money, unless he had earned it in murky dealings. They suspected Walter Dias' activities of being largely of a shady nature, but they could not prove it. Later, they said he used the blanket for various ends which had nothing to do with drawing birds. And they all laughed. They said he always had done so. Mainly, they said, in Valmares, before the *High Monarch* took him off to London and then to Australia, a continent so vast he had begun to feel trapped, and from where he retraced the Atlantic route on another ship. But they also said that one afternoon, Maria Ema dressed her daughter in a *broderie anglaise* pinafore. They said Walter wanted to take Maria Ema's daughter in the buggy with him, but was prevented by the rest of the Dias family. They said a man hoeing in a field alerted them that Walter was taking the child with him, held tightly on his lap. They said the child was hauled out by Francisco Dias himself, while the buggy was actually moving. They gave an eloquent description of how the child was torn from between the shafts to the sound of Francisco Dias' yells—"Stop, you scoundrel, stop!"—thundering across the fields. But I don't remember that. All I really remember is being lifted up by him when the photo was about to be taken, and how we put our heads together, and how, apart from the difference in age and size, we were identical.

But I couldn't tell him that.

9.

Besides, on that night of rain, he said—"Don't call out, don't move!" And seeing that she remained as if pinned to the headboard, even when the promises began pouring forth from him in a torrent, and he wanted her to respond and to say yes to his offer, and she said nothing, mesmerized by the movements of Walter's lips, to which he kept raising an unlit cigarette, he took her by the hand and led her across the room to the lone mirror. "Come on, don't be afraid"—he said.

It was a tall mirror, slotted in between two columns of drawers, an art nouveau piece that matched neither the wardrobe nor the bed. It hung between two perpendicular volutes, positioned so that the light of an oil lamp would be reflected in the mirror. It had lasted from the 1930s, its oddness frozen in time, purely so that she and Walter Dias could be reflected in it that rainy night. But the lamp did not light both their faces evenly because the flame kept flickering, caught by some draft coming in through the roof tiles. Then he said—"Look, look!" And drawing closer to her, he tried to get both of them within the frame of the mirror. "Look, look!" he said, raising his voice, making the night more dangerous, making her feel guilty because of the risks they were all running. But what was surprising was that he spoke as if unaware this was a reprise of another moment. "God, we're so alike!"—Walter was saying, holding the lamp closer, forgetting all about the photograph he had left with Maria Ema. Or, rather, it was as if Walter had forgotten about everything he had left her because, apart from photographs taken later on with a Kodak, next to the agaves, in which the images were so tiny and indistinct that the people in them resembled dead nestlings or crowds of ants, there had only been the one true photograph, predating all others. But

that night, he seemed not to remember. "We're so alike!" he
kept saying.

The photograph was postcard size and brownish in color,
and in it the child was sitting on Walter's lap, both of them
protected by the arms of a high-backed chair, but Maria Ema
used to hide the photograph where no one would find it. In
the Valmares house she buried it so that only very occasionally
would it resurface among the china and the folds of bed linen,
or else tucked into the back of the Flemish paintings sus-
pended on bits of wire at almost ceiling height, leaning into
the room toward the middle of the table, as if about to hurl
themselves down on us. In the 1950s, she would hide it behind
one of those paintings, then she would move it to another
painting, or change the position of the painting itself. And on
Saturday afternoons, she would climb onto a chair that she
balanced on some steps in order to retrieve the photograph
concealed behind the obliquely hung paintings, and she would
point to her on her uncle's knee. "Uncle Walter Dias!"—Maria
Ema would say. And the child colluded in the secret, in those
hiding places where the photo was forced to skulk amidst the
encroaching multitude.

10.

However, what mattered that night was not Maria Ema's con-
cealments or dissemblings but the existence of a photo in
which soldier Walter was no longer dressed as a soldier, but
was wearing a linen suit and holding the child closely in his

arms, both of them looking at the camera perched on a tripod like the belly of a wading bird, both looking at the same fixed point with the same pale eyes. Those who loved them would say they were the eyes of angels, those who did not that they were like cats' eyes. Later, Adelina Dias would describe them as cheetahs' eyes. But those personal transfigurations were of no importance. It mattered little which animal or angelical family they belonged to. Angels must always feel a longing for the night in which they once were animals, and wild beasts doubt-less dream of the shining day when, in the guise of angels, all creation was theirs to hunt. There was no solution to that double nostalgia. All that mattered was that those two pairs of eyes of indefinable species were looking in the same direction, and during the years preceding Walter's visit on that rainy night, she had always imagined how his body and his cheek must have pressed close to hers and how, for a moment—pos-sibly longer, but for at least the time required for the photo-graph to be taken—she would have been enfolded in his male perfume and would have contaminated him with her sour child's breath. And that was what she wanted to say to Walter Dias on that condensed night, during which something funda-mental was being repeated in front of the mirror, but she did not have the words or the time or the ability. They stood there together, he holding the lamp up in front of his drenched rain-coat and she, by his side, wrapped in the bedspread. "Please, look at what's right there in front of us!"–he said, and he leaned his head against hers, and rain dripped in through the roof, fell on the flagstones outside, making that encounter possible. A repetition of what had happened twelve years earlier, on the day of the photograph. Yes, she knew what was right there in front of them.

In the photograph too they had the same curly hair and their heads were touching. She didn't know how they had ended up going into Matos, the photographer's shop, nor how they had reached Faro, nor could she recall the route taken by the buggy, nor the railway line that traversed the fields. All she could remember was the railway station, with its checkered wall tiles, with its tall beech trees, and the way the train whistled as they set off, the steam exploding into the hot countryside. Indeed, she had no idea how they had left or how they had come back, how they had escaped the vigilance of Francisco Dias and his multitude of sons. She assumed Maria Ema must have come too, that she must have gone with them, and that the three of them fled in the buggy along the narrow road flanked by ripe wheat. Only afterward would they have taken the train. But none of that mattered as they stood before the narrow mirror. What mattered was that for one day, in 1951, the three of them had been together. The two of them were not, therefore, looking at the camera, but at the person who had come with them—Maria Ema Baptista, standing next to the camera covered by a black cloth beneath which the photographer was hunched, and expecting from both of them some courageous act that would never be more than an image. But she did not know if she actually remembered that moment or if it was an invention based on the image. She knew she could still feel the touch of Walter's cheek when he lifted her onto his lap and the camera took the first picture. The two of them caught in that brief splendor, a gentle knocking at the door of an instant eternity. The certainty that, even if the flash were the lightning from a storm, they would always be together. And that was what she wanted to say but could not say on that rainy night, when part of the photograph was being repeated in the mirror.

Tonight, though, in order for Walter to tear his gaze from the floor and walk freely about this room as if walking along a quay, an empty quay, it should be said that the image protected her, when, later, she had to face the rabid dog, the closed door, the enigma of mathematics, the darkness of the house, her first sexual encounter or the interpretation of *The Iliad*. When someone called to her from the far side of the night, and even though no one was expecting her, she went toward that call. She ran that risk, defied the yawning mountain pass that opened up between the steep slopes of the void. That image protected her, that photograph of Walter shown to her briefly, amidst almanacs and soup tureens, wrapped in brown paper, hidden at the bottom of boxes and behind pictures. Afterward, long afterward, she remembered seeing it among the silverware, when Custódio Dias knew Walter Dias would never again return. By then, the Americans were already racing toward the moon, and she was twenty years old and sleeping soundly on such various pillows as sand dunes and the seats of cars. In other words, she had become the legitimate daughter of soldier Walter. But all that happened long after the rainy night.

II.

"You're frozen!"—he said, leading her back to the bed and sitting her down on it still wrapped in the bedspread. "Tell me about you, about what you do?"

And lit by the oil lamp he was holding, Walter walked over to her desk, asking her if she had any talent for drawing. He leafed through notebooks, unpiled the piles of books, turned to her and said, satisfied—"At least our handwriting's similar." And then he went over to the wardrobe and opened it and slowly riffled through her clothes, though the light of the oil lamp barely penetrated that far. And she saw him there, in his light-colored raincoat, which she knew was drenched with rain, but which he did not take off, and she wished he would take it off, just for a moment, just to avoid the feeling that, though he was there, he was really en route to somewhere else, but she could not ask him anything. And he closed the wardrobe, far more noisily than he should have, because the rain had slackened at that moment and his footsteps had become audible again. Besides, when he came back from the wardrobe, his eyes seemed paler, and it occurred to her that he would not bother to try to tread softly anymore. And for a moment, she thought he was about to do something inappropriately loud, make a rebellious gesture or a noise that would wake those asleep, that would get them all out of their beds, the occupants of the west room, the children, the grandfather, as well as Blé and Alexandrina, the foreman and his wife, and the three mules, and the few chickens and rabbits, who would all come scurrying from their houses and hutches if Walter refused to tread softly. And that would be too terrible, and she covered her face with her hands so that it would not happen. But he came over and sat at the foot of her bed; his eyes were their normal color again, although his eyelids were red, as was the rest of his face. "It's all right, we've still got time. Over there, you'll have a wardrobe just for your clothes, and completely different clothes too. Warm clothes, so you can cope with the cold. On the way to university, you'll see girls playing snowballs, their fur hoods pulled so far down over their noses, you can barely see their eyes"—he said, smiling again.

But it wasn't true, we didn't have time.

Besides, he himself shook the lamp and saw that there couldn't be much more time and that soon he would have to take off his shoes again and go down the stairs, vanishing like a shadow that had never been. "Until now, I've never given you anything..."—he said again, trying not to make any noise as he replaced the lamp on the dressing table.

The lamp had returned to its proper place. She too had returned to her proper place, leaning against the headboard. At that point, she wanted to say—Wait! But she couldn't. Perhaps because it seemed so simple and easily enumerated, she wanted to tell him about the most palpable legacy he had left her, she wanted to say how, until the age of fifteen, she had grown up accompanied by his army kit. Because then he would understand. Before he went back down the damp stairs, she had to explain to Walter Dias how a handful of rags and eyelets could constitute the person who had worn them, and how that person could remain in the house and provide company and protection until some force or some person undid it, and even then, some fundamental part would still remain. So he could come into her room, laugh and sit down wherever he chose, with no need to give her anything else. On the contrary, she was the one who was indebted to him.

12.

Yes, before that encounter dissolved into nothing, it was vital that she tell him that his uniform had been kept in the wardrobe in the room where she slept. The geography of confusion and chance had ended up placing it in that very room, wide enough to be a living room, and in which the wardrobe now swayed on the farthest wall. And she would have listed everything piece by piece, the rucksack, the boots, the gaiters, the uniform, the overcoat, the cap, the canteen, the scarf and the belt, all of which was tantamount to having the whole of Walter inside the wardrobe. The uniform and cap, in particular, had remained hanging in the darkness like a person waiting day and night for a visitor to come. The daughter slept only yards from the uniform, separated from it by the opaque door. But his daughter knew where the key was and what it was for. She used to slip it into the keyhole, turn it, and then the soldier's body would appear. She calculated that she was barely taller than the sleeve of the overcoat. She would climb into the wardrobe to measure herself against the sleeve. As I said, the daughter often used to go and see these clothes hanging in the wardrobe until, one day, how I don't know, the moths got to them. Suddenly, a voracious colony of moths moved in and devoured the clothes, and when Alexandrina realized they had made a nest there and that this was the source of all the other larvae infesting the clothes in the rest of the house, the overcoat, uniform and hat were carried out into the garden and buried beneath the loquat tree as if they were evidence of a crime. "Bury them good and deep!"—said Alexandrina, and Blé dug deeper and deeper, as if the uniform were an animal with flesh that would rot. Maria Ema was there and she had let them cover the uniform with earth. For a long time afterward, the daughter would hear the spade thudding down on the cloth, on the body of the cloth, and Maria Ema never saying a word. Then they gathered up the rest of the inheritance Walter had left her and took it away.

Wait—she wanted to say.

During the years that followed, they had let time fade and wear away and transform all those things into bits of objects scattered on the ground, assimilated into it, until they had taken on the same color and substance of the earth. But she wanted to tell him that there were some objects that did not disappear, that merely ceased to be material or to have any weight and became instead a memory. They became an invisible fluid entering and leaving the invisible body of the person, becoming incorporated into the circulation of the blood and into the caverns of the memory, to remain lodged there in the very depths of life, persisting alongside it, and all he needed to do that night was to hold up the oil lamp to the body of his daughter in her nightshirt, with the bedspread wrapped around her, to confirm that those objects still lived on inside her head. In silence, with no words to express it, she had stored away those things that had been her inheritance, preserving them entire and intact as beetles inside a pyramid. If Walter were to hold the lamp up to her head, he would see that inside it she had preserved his black gaiters, the enamel canteen, the white scarf, the brown rucksack, the gray flannel uniform and the woolen greatcoat with its long sleeves. And that was what she would have wanted to say to him.

She should have told Walter—who one moment had set the lamp down on the bedside table and the next was holding it up near her head, as if he could not get a close enough look at her, or as if he wanted to set fire to what he saw—that she had not witnessed the destruction of that part of her inheritance with indifference, but rather with the impotence of those who know the earth is the impatient resting place of all it engenders. Children of tender years know that, just as they know everything about death and life. Then they forget. She knew it from the instant Walter's rucksack began to be one with the grass by the wall, at the far end of the mound, and the fact she had acquired that knowledge through Walter's possessions bound her to another soil of an unfamiliar color, but which she knew was waiting for her like a kind and peaceful land where she would experience utter rest. She knew all this from Walter's dispersed possessions. And she wanted to tell him, so that he would stop making promises about expenses, about savings and investments, about glorious places where she would find mortarboards complete with tassels just like the ones worn by those little statues of wise owls, and about liberal professions in liberal worlds, but she could not move her tongue, she could not say a word, she who had brought him there by sheer force of thought. Now, after a hard, lashing downpour, the rain was falling softly, and it was then that Walter realized the lamp might be a liability.

"Listen!"—he said, turning the flame as low as it would go.

13.

They heard the door of the west room close. They heard the sound of asymmetrical footsteps emerging out of the dark. Slow, unmistakable, like two wings dragging along the ground, one heavier and more thickly feathered, more earthbound, the other smaller, lighter, rhythmically beating the air, like a watch, a mechanism, an alarm clock. The regular steps approached and stopped by the landing. And the frightened voice—"Is there anyone up there?" Now they were coming up, one step, another step, both feet on the same stair. And then the flashlight beam sweeping the floor under the door, and then that long moment during which Walter hid the flame of the oil lamp with his hands, and that eternity of doubt until Custódio started slowly going back down with powerful, asymmetric, regular steps, back down the stairs, ticktocking along the corridor to the west room. Yes, that was where Maria Ema slept. And wrapped in the bedspread that was sticky with damp, sticky with burned oil and sticky too with the knowledge that she had engendered all this by sheer force of will, Walter Dias' daughter remembered the thing she had hidden under the mattress, and although she didn't know what to do with it, nor on whom to turn it, she thought she should show it to Walter, so that he would realize he could leave in peace and disappear in turn along the corridor, unconcerned, because nothing would be lost on her, because she would always be safe even in the farthest-flung places, and that was why she did not need him to be there, did not need him to run any risks for her, and thinking that, almost as if she were sleepwalking, she reached head and body between the two mattresses and drew out a dark metal object which she placed before Walter's oil lamp.

And since Walter Dias had again turned up the flame and was looking in surprise at the object his daughter was holding in her hands, it was only natural that, for a moment, he should have thought she was pointing it at him because it was, after all, a gun. It was the Smith revolver.

But it wasn't true, she wasn't pointing it at him.

She just wanted to let him know he could leave, at peace with his life and his conscience, that was all. And in order to show him how well she was protected, she opened the chamber of the gun and began slipping a few metal objects into the cylinders, even though that repetitive gesture made her realize that what she was doing must seem ridiculous and stupid, or even pathetic, like in a scene from a Danny Kaye film. And at that moment, Walter grabbed his daughter's wrist to take the gun from her. "Don't be silly, give me that!"—he said, much more loudly than was sensible, with the flame burning green on what remained of the oil, much more brightly than was sensible, aware that at least someone in that house, a lame man, was not asleep. And she cocked and uncocked the gun again and again, so that he would understand that she was afraid of nothing and of no one, for this was the night on which she had managed both to be born and to say farewell, like the mayfly described in her zoology book, in the chapter on insects of the genus *Ephemera*. Then he himself lowered her arm.

"Good God, what have we done to you?"—he said, somewhat calmer, his gaze darker. However, either because of her decision to get out the gun or because there were the beginnings, inside the house, of a few loud drips falling, which meant that the protective curtain of rain was showing signs of disintegrating, Walter Dias started saying—"Keep calm now, let's just stay nice and calm. We'll go far away from here and everything will be all right. Put that away where you found it. Come on." And he made her lie down and covered her with the blanket and stroked her hair for the first time, for the only time, for the last time in her life. Then he took off his shoes, doused the wick and began going down the stairs. Exactly as she had imagined, exactly as she had wanted, as was happening in the film she herself was making, he had visited her secretly, unbeknownst to anyone, so as not to wound or harm anyone. "Wait"—she wanted to say.

———

Walter Dias could go down the stairs in peace, like a shadow slipping along the wall. He had deliberately let her keep the gun this time. In 1951, he had forgotten to take it with him when he left to join the *High Monarch* in London, and it had become the most important object of all. And during those years, no one had seen it, although some had touched it, making it part of the invisible places and objects that existed inside the house. No one mentioned it, no one seemed to give it any importance, apart from Walter's daughter.

Yes, at the time, there were rooms in the Valmares house inhabited only by furniture, so tall and so dark it seemed to have come from another planet. In a house built as a home for a large family, there were no single beds. You went straight from a cradle adorned in a cloud of organdy to beds that resembled the deck of a ship, and in those beds children were assailed by terrifying dreams. They would dream that they were falling helplessly, that they were lost between the air and the water, between another sea and another earth, and no one could save them, and they would cry out, believing that somewhere there must be some sure salvation, some safe haven. They would cry out for someone to hear. But she had never needed to shout or call out, because she had always had a place of safety and something with which to protect herself. She knew that it lay between the straw mattress and the woolen mattress. The Smith revolver that had belonged to soldier Walter. Walter's daughter would lie curled up on that revolver, staring into the darkness, immune to the terror of the darkness surrounding her.

14.

Because the darkness was a creature.

The darkness rose up near the railway line, then advanced, circled and approached, stalking her, brushing against her body like a prowling wolf, touching the body of Walter's daughter with its rancid breath. And lying in the middle of the bed, that same bed, in the middle of the immense night that beat on the very edges of the sea, she would stay absolutely still, waiting for the darkness to open its mouth, to lick her with its stinking tongue and devour her, beginning with her head. Huddled in the middle of the bed, Walter's daughter would offer up her head, but she did so only in order to find out if Walter Dias' gun would or would not speak out against the vile power of the darkness. The gun was right under her body, she could feel it between the two mattresses. The night creature saw the gun gleaming under her body. The vile creature had X-ray vision, it knew where the power lay, the power to exterminate darkness and evil, and the foul creature of the night that visited Walter's daughter knew that if it so much as touched her head, it would immediately be exterminated by her father's revolver. Then, in the midst of the darkness, Walter's daughter would draw her legs up to a sitting position, and the heavy metal revolver would act of its own accord. The revolver would turn on the beast circling her, which would then leap the surrounding walls of the salt-corroded house and vanish, with an extraordinary howl of silence, into the distance, far, far away, where the pale waves broke on the shore. The daughter would coil about the place where the gun was kept, she would roll up like a ball of thread, like a small guard dog, hugging that source of power left behind, forgotten, by soldier Walter. "Wait," she wanted to say and could have said.

She could have told him that there was a time when Francisco Dias' house was crowded. That in it labored six sons and three daughters-in-law, a daughter, a son-in-law, and three grandchildren—the daughter and the first two sons of Maria Ema and Custódio. There was a maid, her husband, their children, and five or six day laborers, who were there by dawn and were dismissed if they weren't. That, during those years, the early mornings were devoted to distributing tasks, provisions, food and hay, followed by much human toing and froing entirely dictated by the needs of the animals and their toing and froing, for the animals were very like people in their moods and subterfuges and sudden veerings off in the wrong direction, and when this happened, Francisco Dias' sons would yell at the animals and bicker among themselves. Apart from these confrontations, however, they were a silent brotherhood, on the point of going their separate ways, although as far as Francisco Dias was concerned, it was the most united of families. He believed his house to be a solid enterprise, a production unit created in the likeness of a state, and he ruled over it much as a parsimonious governor might. In the name of frugality, economy and production, in the name of a serious, miserly, united and indivisible future, from which so far only one member had escaped, Walter.

The production unit led by Francisco Dias woke two hours before dawn. As in an empire where the ears of the emperor are everywhere and his energy is transmitted through the very atmosphere, the house woke when Francisco Dias woke. "Time to get up!"—he would bawl, standing in the dark court-yard in his shirtsleeves, washing his face, banging the copper basin on the flagstones so that he could be heard even in the attic, and striding about the house in his hobnail boots. The cockerels would start crowing at that point too, and work would begin. At the entrance to the house, opposite the map of the world, there was a poster of a cockerel with its beak open, crowing out a radiant dawn. On those winter mornings of 1953, everything that could be woken up was woken up.

15.

Walter's daughter woke up with the rest of the house, but she was laboring on something else.

She would leap barefoot to the floor, stick her head and body between the mattresses and crawl cautiously in, stretching her arm as far as she could until she could feel the gun and grasp it. It was wrapped in a rust-stained cloth, and next to it lay three heavy yellow objects, three metal acorns, three gold-colored pendants which she would examine carefully. They were bullets. As the volume of sound intensified inside the house, she would place the gun on one side, the bullets on the other. She would arrange the bullets in an arc, in a straight line, in a combination of two and one, with the points innermost or outermost, or all three together. She would pick up the gun, a heavy weight even when she held it in both hands, an inviolable object, with no entrance and no exit. Until one day it ceased to be inviolable. Suddenly, part of the gun moved, it swung free from the back of the weapon, the weapon had ears, a tail, a mouth, the gun opened and closed. Inside the heart of the weapon were four orifices into which the bullets could be fitted. One by one, Walter's daughter slipped them in. To get them out, the acorns would have to make the journey in reverse, because she didn't want them to stay inside. And then one morning, she left them in. It didn't matter. If the mechanism spun around, it must be possible to make them come out of the mouth, but if one of them did come out, that would be a gunshot, like the shot that killed the partridge, wounded the old dog or the thief on the road. That was what a gun was for. Otherwise, the powerful creature of the night darkness would have no reason to be afraid when it found the gun hidden between the mattresses. She would have to pull the trigger and aim at some surface. The bedroom wall was not sufficiently animated. She could, though, go downstairs and use the gun on an actual person.

Who? On those cold mornings in 1954, Walter's daughter chose Maria Ema. In the middle of the corridor, still in her dressing gown, she would receive the shot in the V-shaped opening immediately above her breasts. Covered in blood, like the old dog and the partridge, Maria Ema would cry out, flinging open her dressing gown. Her shouts would be followed by Custódio's, by those of Joaquim Dias, Manuel Dias and their wives, by those of the other three Dias children, of Francisco Dias and the laborers, who were still outside at that hour, and they would all converge on Walter's daughter in order to punish her, while Maria Ema rose from her chair unscathed, inviolable, untouchable, still wrapped in the gray dressing gown with the big yellow roses on it. Immortal, like the characters in cartoons.

Then, sitting on her bed, Walter's daughter would turn the gun on Custódio Dias as he limped toward the animals waiting to be yoked to the carts. She would get him as she heard him walking along the path, leaving in his wake the regular asymmetry that distinguished him from his brothers laboring in the courtyard. And nothing happened to him either. From her bed she would hear a boom, see the thread of blood, see him fallen on the ground, and everyone would rush to save him, but he was already saved, and in the midst of the men dragging plows and pitchforks, voices would be raised against Walter's daughter. Then they would all look at her and point at her with goads, pitchforks and poles, even though Custódio was still alive and well, surrounded by his saviors. The same would happen with her brothers who seemed always to be asleep. She could go over to their cradles and shoot the metal acorns into their white bellies. Their diapers would be stained red as pomegranate juice, as red as the edge of the flag unfurling next to the cockerel in the poster, as red as her own wounds when she fell. Her brothers would be undone by her golden acorns. And yet, even before she could inflict a wound, they would be surrounded by a crowd of people who did not love each other, but who united in the face of any danger, which is why no one could touch them or hurt them or kill them. So she used to think.

———

But if Walter Dias' daughter turned the gun on herself, on her own chest and belly, no one would come. No one would rush to pick her up from the floor; there would be no need. She would suffer no pain, she would not bleed. The golden bud would leave the mouth of the revolver and explode in her head like a silently opening carnation the color of fire, only without any flames. Lying down or curled up on the bed, Walter's daughter would go back to sleep, aware of the laborious life going on beneath her, but no one came upstairs, no one worried about her, they left her there in a state of marvelous neglect. And no one gave a thought to Walter's daughter. She would lie there forever on her side, in the warm, damp wave of the bed, protected by the quiet of the big room, for a long, long time. Calmly, eternally, as sweet and gentle as a sea of urine spreading over the mattress. As it cooled, though, the puddle would drive her out, she already knew that nothing in life lasts, not even that solitary morning sense of well-being. She would pull the gun out from beneath the sheet. She was still thinking that if each of those bullets had gone into the gun, they must also come out. The puddle was seeping into her body, penetrating it. Sitting beside the hundredth puddle, she wielded the gun with every ounce of her strength. Day by day, that weapon she could not discharge waited between the mattresses. But one day, when she least expected it, the revolver opened and offered up from inside its metal belly the nest in which the bullets were lodged. One by one, she removed the bullets. That was how her room was on those winter mornings in 1954—That was what she wanted to tell him.

16.

She used to think about Maria Ema, about Custódio Dias and Francisco Dias. Did they know she slept with a revolver under her mattress? That the gun lay hidden between the mattresses day and night? Yes, they must know, but no one, it seemed, had thought to find out. Perhaps they left it there as a gift, a suggestion or a challenge, in order that she or all of them might take a risk, or in order to create a lacuna, a disappearance, a dazzling, unexpected change. They had left Walter Dias' revolver beneath her body so that they would all run that risk— the irrepressible desire for tragedy that exists in the heart of every family. As if the ever-growing tension required a detonator. It must be obvious. So many people changed the bed and changed the sheets. The wool in the mattress was regularly replaced and the straw in the lower mattress turned. Alexandrina, Maria Ema, Adelina Dias and the sisters-in-law all knew of the existence of the revolver and the bullets. So why did no one see them?

For that reason, on the night Walter Dias visited her, the bullets and the revolver were out of sight, and he wanted to take the gun away from her on that rainy night, he wanted to take the gun with him, but she realized that if he took it, when Walter did disappear, he might disappear entirely. He even said to her—"Don't be silly!" But she couldn't give him back the weapon. Giving it back would be like handing over the fragile link that bound his existence to hers. She could give him back the album of birds, the brown photograph, his army kit, or the scene around the kitchen table when he returned from India,

43

but not the revolver. It was part of her dearest inheritance and that was the reason why, at that point, she could not give it up, not even to Walter.

17.

Naturally, she could not have explained it like that, as she would have liked to have done once Custódio's footsteps had disappeared back into the west room, and Walter Dias finally understood that his daughter could not give up the revolver he himself had used, but which he had long since forgotten, and on which, ever since she was a little girl, she had slept, just in case. And then he said she could keep the gun for as long as she liked. He said this so that the night would end peaceably, as it did–"You can even keep it with you in Ontario. Even when I give you that present I talked about—an airplane trip to La Guardia and a boat trip slipping slowly down the Hudson River, beneath the Statue of Liberty. But first, we'll head for Muskoke County to hear the loons laughing. You'll love the way that bird chuckles. But, of course, you can keep that thing for as long as you like..." Yes, she could keep the gun, Walter understood, he understood everything on that rainy night. He even said it had been a great shame to have exchanged her for India, for tropic birds and for other birds of passage, for the complete absence of birds on long voyages, for the golden waves, for the ballast of foam as the ship sailed along. He had been promised that they would sail down the Suez Canal and come back via the Cape. As well as the possibility of sailing between Mormugão and Karachi, and much,

much more. Those were the voyages he had exchanged her for, as if there were no other destinations, no other seas, and then he had regretted it—"What did they tell you?"

It was getting late and, just as she wanted, just as she was asking him to do, without actually saying, he would go quietly down the stairs in his stocking feet, in the light-colored rain-coat still damp from the rain. But first, as I said, Walter Dias stroked her hair and tucked her in. Only then did he remove the glass from the oil lamp and blow out the flame.

18.

But tonight he stops at the door and does not come in, he does not take off his shoes, he does not shut the door behind him, nor does he pick up a lamp, as if he did not want his face to be seen or as if he had come to ask forgiveness again, for no reason. There never was any reason. It was as if chance had wanted to demonstrate precisely that—because his blanket wandered from post office to post office for ten months and finally arrived today in São Sebastião de Valmares, and, at first, it was hard to comprehend how a parcel with the sender's address and that of the addressee so blurred by stains and surrounded by messages, some of them illegible, could ever have reached its destination. Maria Ema called Custódio Dias and the two of them stood examining the package, then she handed him the kitchen scissors and they opened it together, and only then passed the contents on to Walter's daughter. The blanket was unfolded and spread out on the ground, and she wished he could come back and visit her again so she could tell him that she had inherited the rainy night with all that it contained imprinted on its magma, which is why it was so unfair of the man to have written that ironic comment about himself on the card—*I leave to my niece, as sole inheritance, this soldier's blanket.* And now he approaches slowly, he does not speak to her, he utters not a word, he has nothing to say.

Besides, even if the night of 1963 had not existed, Walter's daughter would always have had enough to make up a valuable inheritance. The image she had constructed of him was her inheritance. When Walter had started to take his shoes off on the landing, she already knew him, and everything she knew about him was good, although she hadn't managed to say so, for during the encounter she hadn't said a single word, despite his insistence. "Go on, say something, even something cruel..."—he had said, at last, when he was tucking the sheet around her and stroking her head where she kept her cheetah's gaze. Where she kept her inheritance. On that rainy night, she already knew that a life did not belong solely to the person it belonged to, but also to the person to whom that life was recounted. She knew Walter's life was not just hers, it belonged to many people, because, in Valmares, everyone imagined his life and told the others what they had imagined. Walter existed in the others too and each one had a little piece of him, which they talked about with gusto, as if they owned all of Walter. The Dias family partook of him like the Host, they fed off his life like someone eating a sweet dessert, cold. She had known for years that when Walter was still a child, he had taken over the old buggy that had belonged to Joaquina Glória, and that he himself had repaired it and painted it, and that he was in the habit of hitching a light-colored mare to it and tearing off along the roads while his brothers labored from sunrise to sunset. Gradually, she found out that Walter never worked, regardless of the threats and privations doled out by Francisco Dias. That ever since he was eleven years old, he had refused to collaborate, and instead would sleep all morning, then get up and set off along unknown roads, taking shortcuts through the wheat fields where he would get lost. Francisco Dias, the Dias brothers, his sister Adelina, his brother-in-law, his sisters-in-law, his brothers' girlfriends, the foreman Blé and his wife Alexandrina, who lived in the house at the rear, the laborers who came, went or stayed on after sunset in the 1950s, all have some story to tell about Walter's life. His daughter, however, would shut herself up alone with these archaic narratives, modifying and reconstructing them; she may not have had all the words, but she understood. And that is why all of that would still have been a fundamental part of her inheritance, even if the night visit had never taken place. The album of drawings, the sleeve of his overcoat or the revolver would have meant nothing if Walter had not existed. She could see him disappearing into the wheat fields, she could see him when he was the same height as the wheat, she could imagine his boyish footsteps crunching over the stubble, zigzagging away so as not to be caught. She could imagine.

19

But the episode she had inherited intact, the one that introduced all the others and formed the basis of the film of his return from India which she had been piecing together since 1951,
was very precise and did not require any alteration or development. It had a life of its own, carving out a shape for itself in
space. Walter was twelve years old and Francisco Dias had said
to him—"Look, you're no more important than any of the others. Pick up your basket like everyone else." The task involved
filling the basket with manure and handing the full basket up
to be emptied into the carts. João Dias, fourteen, Inácio, fifteen, Luís, seventeen, and Manuel, nineteen, were all in the
depths of the dungheap, filling baskets. Custódio, twenty-
three, and Joaquim, twenty, took the baskets and tipped them
out into the back of the mule carts. In their haste to fill the
baskets, the Dias brothers, both those above and those below,
were becoming plastered with dung, and Walter looked down
into the dungheap and refused to climb in. He was forced to
do so. Swept along on a current of obedience that was stronger
and more imperative than the voice of Francisco Dias, they all
obeyed, using short pitchforks to fill the baskets and then lifting the baskets up to the edge of the pit. They picked up the
ripe, steaming, fertile, rotten dung in which they themselves
were covered, as if they were part of it and did not mind being
part of it. But Walter, the youngest, who had been pushed into
the pit, would not pick up the pitchfork and refused to budge.
"Go on, get stuck in it like your brothers!" Hearing their father's shouts, the others worked faster still. The faster they

worked, their faces turned to the muck, the closer Walter moved to the wall of the pit in order to clamber up the side.

His father hit him with a pitchfork to stop him from climbing up, while Custódio and Joaquim kept loading the cart faster and faster and the others dug deeper and deeper. And Walter, clawing at the wall of dung, confronted his father, crying out in his yet unbroken voice. A small boy, with straw-colored hair, shouting loudly, defying his father from the middle of the dungheap. And the cry—"You stop that, Senhor Francisco Dias!"—came from Alexandrina, who was passing nearby carrying a basin of clean laundry. "You wouldn't get away with that if Joaquina Glória was alive!" And setting down her basin, possibly on the dung-strewn ground, and at the risk of having to wash the clothes all over again, Alexandrina managed to wrench the pitchfork from Francisco Dias' hand, tugging first at the handle and then at Francisco Dias himself so that he lost his balance and nearly fell. He tried to grab the end again, but she wouldn't let him, and all the while the Dias brothers continued to fill and empty baskets, while she held the pitchfork up above her head. It was thanks to her intervention, thanks to that humanitarian gesture on the part of Alexandrina, maid and washerwoman, recounted ad nauseam by Alexandrina herself during the 1950s, that the daughter had learned the details of that day of battle. And Alexandrina always used to end by saying—"Francisco Dias was pointing the pitchfork straight at him, and your uncle lifted up his shirt and bared his chest to him, screaming wildly up at his own father. Your uncle was always so odd, so prickly, so rebellious." Then

Alexandrina would stop talking. Walter Dias existed then between the courtyard and the dungheap, in flight from the dungheap. She had inherited that image of him confronting the sharp prongs of a pitchfork.

20.

When he came up the stairs, and while she waited for the door to inch open, just a little, just enough for him to slip in, she had long ago inherited the Valmares household of the 1940s, some of whom she had even known. She could imagine the silent Dias brothers enjoying the battles between their father and his youngest son, watching, waiting for some drastic action, some act of violence that would put an end to Walter's idle ways. She had inherited the image of some country lads leaning against the wall, watching the battle. Blé, the foreman, had told her about it. Walter Dias was climbing onto the buggy and Francisco Dias was standing in the middle of the courtyard, screaming—"Over my dead body..." The father with his arms outstretched, his youngest son leaning over the shafts, confronting him, and the other sons all around, waiting. João, Inácio, Luís, Manuel, Joaquim and Custódio. And Adelina was shouting—"Watch out, he might kill you, Pa!" Perhaps. Perhaps Walter would pull on the reins, the mare would rear up and the father be crushed beneath the wheels. Perhaps they would have to order a black coffin bearing a red cross, perhaps they would have to place the crushed body of their father inside that coffin and hold a tearful funeral, by a grave made by murder. Perhaps the Faro police would come for Walter with a pair of heavy handcuffs. Perhaps all of that would happen at the moment of confrontation. Perhaps.

But, according to Blé, Custódio came up behind his father, the two of them wrestled, their hats rolling on the ground, and Francisco Dias, red-faced, his clothes awry, was eventually dragged into the house by his eldest son. With the way ahead free, Walter released the brake, flicked the reins, and the buggy moved off. No one quite knew where he was going. He used to come back in the evening, sometimes at nightfall, with the lamp on the buggy lit, and he would be whistling. The white mare would be exhausted from trotting along the tarmac roads. Ah, if only the mare could speak, if only she could say where Walter took her. Women, that's what he went after, after traffickers, after all kinds of vices, perhaps he went after alcoholic drinks that left no smell on the breath. But what alcoholic drinks did that? What women did not give you the pox? One day, the foreman, Blé, followed him surreptitiously, but it was very hard to follow in the tracks of Francisco Dias' youngest son. Blé had never managed to do as Francisco Dias wanted him to—to follow him in the carriage. The carriage was much slower than the buggy and attracted attention wherever it went. Everyone knew Francisco Dias' carriage, Blé would say to himself.

The foreman would never stop to talk, but he was always ready to talk to Walter's daughter whenever she would trail after him—"You should have seen your uncle..." Her uncle was learning how to draw birds, he was going to draw them and sell them. Later, he was bolder about it, he bought cartridge paper, paints, pencils, and other implements and would sit down to draw, then frame his drawings out in the yard, as if he were a poor picture-framer. Francisco Dias' youngest son sold his drawings of birds and refused to work. The confrontation had changed, because Walter Dias was now seventeen and he would tell the others loudly that if they didn't let him use the buggy, he would set off on foot and never come back, and no one knew whether he would or not. Sometimes Francisco Dias hated him and only put up with him because he knew that in every group of sons there was always one reprobate whom nature had nurtured in the bosom of a close family so that the balance would be maintained, so that it was clear that evil did not only exist elsewhere. A running sore out of which the imbalance oozed, along with the shame of that imbalance, and thus each family should be grateful for its reprobate. When that imbalance was concentrated in one individual, it encouraged the others to be discreet and well-balanced. The united Dias brothers, the hardworking, exemplary Dias brothers working their father's land ever since they were children, an example to other families, buying up for next to nothing scraps of stony ground, which, in less than a year, by dint of sheer hard work, they would transform into fields of beans.

Yes, there must be some kind of deal made with destiny, a sort of exchange between the profane and the sacred. Francisco Dias let Walter Dias do as he pleased so that his other sons, to compensate, would bond together. Let him go to hell his own way. The lower he sank, the more united the others would be.

In the Valmares house, evil, the inevitable evil, was all concentrated in that one son. All he had to do, then, was to isolate him, watch his movements, but not talk to him much or explain anything. She became familiar with the calendar of disgrace. In 1940, through Walter, God had introduced imbalance into the house of Francisco Dias. That imbalance had lasted until 1946 and resumed after his return from India in the summer of 1951. It had only stopped when he set sail on the *High Monarch* in a city called London. Was that very far away? His daughter would follow Blé across the fields, but she never spoke, never asked any questions, she just listened. She liked to imagine that other face.

21.

Francisco Dias used to talk about Walter too.

It was clear to him that a black cloud hung over his youngest son. He would say so to anyone who would listen when he had free time on Sundays, before dozing off, though never speaking directly to Walter's niece, but then he never spoke to her anyway. He did not, however, conceal from her the difference between Walter and his other sons, should she care to hear, if she could hear. She walked among them as if she were deaf, and he didn't care whether she heard him or not. Francisco Dias put it all down to school, the place where, in his opinion, the life of a man was not only shaped but also summarized and foretold. This is how he explained it.

All his other children had been taught by energetic men, hard, tough and irreproachable, men who never allowed children to fidget, who dealt out punishments and never smiled, but imposed order and tried to inculcate obedience and thus make every child into a good worker. The school in São Sebastião had four windows that faced onto the street. At each of them there was nearly always a child wearing a donkey's head, complete with cloth ears and prominent teeth. But behind the big mouth, the child's face was easily identifiable. The whole of São Sebastião would know which child had been punished. The masks ceased being masks and became the children themselves. The shame of the children. And shame had always been an essential element in the creation of obedience, especially during the diligent 1930s. All his children, including Adelina Dias, had experienced that rigorous, formative, punitive discipline, as was only right. "All of them, apart from Walter"—Francisco Dias would say, and sometimes, his feet in espadrilles, the hobnail boots laid aside, he couldn't even manage to doze off in his mahogany chair. And all because of his youngest son. Walter's niece would be watching.

Yes, unlike the others, the youngest son was destined to be taught by an incompetent newcomer, a small man with a beardless face, who would light a fire on top of the desk and burn paper and the heads of matches, or alcohol and cotton wool inside bottles. Every so often, he would take the children up into the gray São Sebastião hills and tell them to observe nature, to spy on the animals. He told them to measure the course of the sun with a stonemason's rule, obliged them to go to school at night in order to explain eclipses to them, had them record such pointless things as the different positions of a horse's legs when it ran and when it walked. He didn't teach them anything. He himself made special tubes through which he would have the children look at birds, when all the children needed to know about birds was which were useful and which were not and which set men a good example by their habits, and then to write this down in a neat hand. But that pervert brought actual birds, alive and dead, into the classroom, where he would open out their wings to show the children the different sorts of feathers, the way the feet were articulated when they landed and when in flight. And that is how Walter first started drawing animals in motion, especially birds. Francisco Dias would tell this to anyone who cared to listen. She listened.

How could she not? She learned that this teacher had been driven out of São Sebastião because of a petition which many had "signed" with a thumbprint. One December night in 1935, they had come for the beardless teacher. The teacher had been forced out of education and had died young, having nothing else to do, watched as he was on all sides, but meanwhile he had done irreparable harm wherever he had taught. You could see it clearly in the person of Walter.

Francisco Dias remembered being called in to see that frail teacher, just to be told by him what extraordinary hands Walter had, hands that drew as if the memory of nature were concealed beneath their fingertips. A truly remarkable talent. And although at the time, Walter and the others were more often than not drawing St. Sebastian and Our Lady of Sorrows, Francisco Dias suspected that those drawings were just a cover for the children to continue drawing entire animals, including their reproductive organs, an excuse for his son to draw birds. He also discovered that while they did not put the saints' names beneath their drawings of saints, their drawings of birds appeared complete with their Latin nomenclature. Francisco Dias himself had written to the police commissioner telling him of his suspicions, and he himself had instigated the petition of thumbprints, and it was on his initiative that the teacher had disappeared. But for various miseducated children it had been too late. Too late for his son, Walter, who escaped the house in order to go and draw birds.

Yes, she had found out how Walter used to lie down on the ground and wait for the birds to land, sometimes he would catch them in baskets and cages from which he would subsequently release them, but first, he would reproduce them on paper, copying their feathers and their shapes, giving their eyes in particular a special life. It was as if the wretched sparrows could speak, as if the thrushes were laughing, all because of those lines he added to their eyes or because of the way he drew their raised tails and their spread wings. One day, Adelina Dias had yelled—"Pa, these aren't birds, they're people coupling!" Francisco Dias had already suspected as much. How else could he possibly sell those drawings if there wasn't some other motive behind it? Francisco Dias simply could not believe that, instead of Flemish landscapes, people would want to buy drawings of birds—ducks, doves, pigeons, flycatchers— and that they would even commission them. "Pa, he's drawing two parrots kissing each other! Pa, they're touching beaks!"

Francisco Dias would tell people, helped by Adelina. Walter's daughter knew all this on that rainy night. For some years she used to imagine Walter drawing the birds which she now owned.

22.

But Francisco Dias did not always doze off during his free hour on Sunday. Sometimes he would receive his friends and, together, they would invoke the recent War in which they had not fought. Walter's daughter would sit down with her back to them and listen.

In the 1940s, the Dias brothers had been afraid they might become involved in actual battles, especially those of them who were still doing their military service and might, from one moment to the next, become part of an expeditionary force. Bad years, lean years. No rain, no manure, years of wind and dust, hot years, but for Francisco Dias they had been good years. This is why—Francisco Dias sold olive oil and flour at high prices and in small quantities, as if he were selling gold, and he sold only to other sellers, he did so in collaboration with his children and, although they had the opportunity, neither he nor they were ever involved in the black market. They didn't need to be, this was the fruit of their battle against a desert climate, the product of their sweat. In two years, Francisco Dias bought ten plots of stony land and hired a team of laborers to break up the stones with sledgehammers because he didn't have any gunpowder. João and Inácio, who were still in Lagos, would soon be back to come to grips with the land and the lack of manure, to help dig up rocks, fill the dungheap and spread the dung on the earth to produce more, to produce the yellow wheat, the green beans, the golden grain, the laden trees, earth dug by the arms of Dias men, despite the arid climate. What was keeping them? She came to her own conclusions based on what Francisco Dias said. And one September afternoon, they heard a deafening noise and thought the war must have reached Portugal at last. But it turned out to be just a sample gone astray. From the west a plane came hurtling toward the sea, and within seconds, how they never knew, a twin-engined fighter plane with two dead Englishmen strapped in the cabin had crashed in front of Francisco Dias' house. It had landed next to the threshing floor, destroying ten mats of as yet untasted figs. And then they were besieged by the silence of the authorities and by the oilcloths covering the stretchers. Francisco Dias and his friends remembered all these things.

Then Francisco Dias would relax a bit and, over a hand of cards, in the brief Sunday afternoon heat, he would talk. That image had brought with it an extraordinary thought for which he took no responsibility whatever, it just came to him. In place of one of those blond aviators, scorched and dead, in place of one of them, he had seen with remarkable clarity his own son Walter, if Walter had gone to war. Or, rather, if he went. Had he enlisted or had Portugal suddenly decided to participate, sending soldiers from among the new recruits, the war would not have taken any of his other sons, only Walter. Francisco Dias spoke his thought, pleased with himself and with the modest battle he had fought in order to save his youngest son. His reasoning had been lucid and absolutely right.

Yes, if Portugal entered the War, and an expeditionary force was sent, and if Walter was among them, he would, in short, either die or be saved. If Walter died, he could be decorated posthumously, and he himself would receive that medal and someone would come and play a trumpet over Walter's grave. And if he were saved, which was also probable, or at least possible, he would come back a changed man. He was bound to return gaunt, smoke-blackened, debilitated and disciplined, having learned what effort, illness and death meant. He would come back a serious man. He wouldn't go haring off in the buggy anymore, he wouldn't wear out the horse, he wouldn't sing those awful songs, always repeating the same phrases, while he did his drawings–"Charlie, Charlie…"

But Walter could happily go on drawing and making picture frames and filling the house with "Charlie, Charlie…" Toward the end of 1944, in stations and other public places, small black notices began to appear, announcing to the Portuguese: *People of Portugal, Work and Save so that God may spare you from the War!* Which, in a way, was a bit annoying for Francisco Dias, because although the strategy announced in the accompanying leaflet meant he could acquire more plots of stony land, it also meant having to relinquish all hope of seeing his son removed from the house. The real impediment, however, occurred during the week before Walter was due to leave for the barracks in Évora, set, as a barracks should be, in the middle of a vast, barren plain. A suitable place for men being trained for a major war. The impediment took the following form—a week before his son's departure, the buggy returned earlier than usual and Walter jumped down, leaving the mare in the middle of the courtyard, and shouting–"Everyone's saying that the war's over!" Custódio walked over with his asymmetrical gait to steady the buggy. "What do you mean it's over?" And Adelina Dias ran after Francisco Dias, who was taking the horse to the stable. "Pa, the war's over!" Francisco Dias removed a scrap of horse dirt from his hat. "That's a lie, it can't be over, it isn't..."

Francisco Dias told how he had been foiled by fate. He remembered seeing Walter lying flat on his back on the ground, his arms flung wide, joyfully shouting–"The war's over!" That was how his daughter saw him. And she would always have seen him like that, even if that night in 1963 had never existed.

23.

It was still such a relatively recent event that Francisco Dias could still describe the relief he had felt on the night he watched his youngest son depart, leaning out of a carriage window, waving wildly, his hat in his hand, before disappearing into the darkness of the trees that grew alongside the railway line. Francisco Dias' sigh of relief when he got home that night was like the triumphant yelp the night train used to give as it crossed the narrow, sandy plain, regardless of whether there was a war on or not. He had disappeared.

But the railway line went in two directions and occasionally it brought back some of the passengers it had taken away, and five months later, the same carriage, turned to leeward, deposited Walter at Valmares station. And unlike Francisco Dias' imaginings when he had seen those two Englishmen trapped in the cockpit of the plane, Walter seemed even more alive, even more of a man, with muscular arms, sharp features, close-cropped hair, straight, white teeth, his smile even broader. In short, he was different. And with every monthly visit he was even more different.

He would jump down from the train at five o'clock on a Saturday and go back at eight o'clock on a Sunday, and during those barely twenty-four hours of leave, Walter Dias would not rest. He would hitch the white mare to the black buggy and be gone. He would trot along the smooth, flat road that ran parallel with the sea, kicking up the tarmac as he went. Sometimes, he would take off toward the bleak moors, but the steep, potholed roads, flanked by rocky outcrops and carob trees casting sinister shadows, would force him to turn back. He would return to the smoother road where the mare could trot along, mane flying, without stumbling over stones. It was as if he came home only in order to race the buggy. The only brother who looked forward to seeing him was Custódio Dias, who would spend Sunday at the door of the house waiting for him to come back. He would go to the far end of the courtyard to wait for him, he would put away his brother's buggy and take care of his horse. This, according to Francisco Dias, was irresponsibly protective behavior. "Correct me if I'm wrong"—his father would say to Custódio—"but I think the only reason you don't do what he does is because you can't. Don't tell me you want to draw birds too!" The spring of 1946. Custódio would have been thirty-one. Sitting with her back to them, the daughter would calculate the ages of the Dias brothers in relation to Walter's age.

Naturally, Francisco Dias never spoke to her. Perhaps she couldn't even hear. She was almost dumb, she didn't talk, she didn't hear, she didn't know anything, it didn't matter whether Walter's niece heard or not. But sometimes Alexandrina, the foreman's wife, would address herself solely and secretly to Walter's daughter. She would say—"Now your uncle's real problem wasn't birds, it was women. He wore himself out running after them and the problem was they were just as mad about him…" She would turn around and add softly—"But then something awful happened…" Alexandrina would say in the kitchen, sticking the point of the knife into the heart of the potatoes, splitting them in two and hurling them into the pans from which the Dias brothers ate.

Because everyone was waiting for it to happen, for Walter's sexual side to manifest itself, to leave behind it a lighted fuse, to become the subject of scandal, for him to reveal his true personality once and for all, so that his life would be seen as clearly reprehensible, and order would be restored. There was talk of the buggy being tethered outside a particular door, being seen in a certain place, of him racing back, with the mare flecked with foam, from somewhere near Faro. Yes, a man who was a soldier, who painted birds and did no work, was bound to reveal himself through his sexual behavior, because otherwise, the figure would remain incomplete and incomprehensible and no one could rest easy in their beds. And so time passed and, of course, it happened—in Alexandrina's words, more vivid than anyone else's. But the authorized version came from the Dias brothers themselves and it always centered on that Sunday in June.

24.

The daughter found out what happened. The heat was intense on that June Sunday, the dogs were underneath the wooden table, eating, when suddenly they raced past the legs of the Dias brothers and stood barking crazily by the courtyard gate. But the people arriving did not seem to notice the dogs. An open wooden cart was tethered to the ring, and Francisco Dias recognized the people hurrying across the courtyard as Manuel Baptista and his wife, who lived in a house by the roadside, with a rose tree growing by the door, and only later did he notice that behind them came a tall, rather delicate girl, with her hands clasped in front of her. Francisco Dias threw open the door, but Manuel Baptista seemed to have no intention of coming in. As the girl slowly approached, he pointed at her— the brim of her straw hat covering her face and her hands at waist height—as if he did not know her–"I've come here to tell you that your youngest son has put her in the family way." And as everyone said, at every opportunity, and whenever it occurred to them, Baptista added that he had not come there to make demands, but purely so that Francisco Dias should know that the boy had left his seed inside his daughter. And that the seed was growing. The girl was Maria Ema Baptista.

"Yes, her!"—because Manuel Baptista knew it wasn't his fault, but hers, his daughter's. He had no doubt that Maria Ema had jumped up into the buggy and that she herself had lain down on the army blanket on which Walter had sex with women by the roadside. She was the youngest. But she didn't realize it had only happened because Walter hadn't had any luck with her older sisters, Dulce and Quitéria, nor with her cousins, protected from the seductions of his drawing skills by the promise of more serious-minded men who were bound to turn up. The pregnant girl stood there, stunned, wearing a straw hat that made her look even younger than she was, her belly slightly rounded, her short dress hitched up at the front, revealing her knees.

And in order to say something, in the midst of the heat and the violent light out in the courtyard, Francisco Dias, with his napkin still tucked in his shirtfront, had immediately assumed his fatherly role, saying there was no way they could prove his son had been the one to put her in the family way— "How can you prove something like that?" And Manuel Baptista knew he was absolutely right and he asked his wife, whom he, in passing, also blamed, to show what they had brought with them. And from inside the small bag, getting her fingers caught in the handles, his wife drew a bundle of papers which she passed to her husband, and her husband passed them to

Francisco Dias with all the solemnity of someone handing over a cruel testament, and Walter Dias' father shook his head and said that it was, indeed, the work of his son Walter. And he stood there thinking and thinking, still clutching the papers, on that scorching Sunday afternoon, until he could find something else to say, as the father he was—"The problem is, of course, a woman who gives herself to one man will give herself to anyone. She's lost all credit…" "Yes, you're right"—Manuel Baptista agreed—"She's totally discredited herself." But Alexandrina felt sorry for Walter's niece, who seemed so removed from it all, sitting with her back to them, not saying a word, while she and her husband, both of them at once, recounted what had happened.

And that is why Alexandrina walked around the chair and stood in front of Walter's daughter, with the grater in her hand, crumbling, sieving, mashing, with the help of a fork, the flesh of the remaining vegetables. Alexandrina could still see Maria Ema, on that scalding June afternoon, pale and still as a china doll, stunned, as if she had been dropped into the middle of the ocean, not knowing whether to leave the court-yard quickly or slowly. She would soon find out. Without saying a word to each other, the Baptistas unhitched the cart and climbed up, but they wouldn't let their daughter climb up with them. Maria Ema was going to have to pay. She was just beginning to. The cart set off, sides swaying, sending up a cloud of dust, and Maria Ema started walking behind. She ran along after the carriage, never reaching it, in the trail of dust.

———

She had heard the story dozens of times, with slight variations, but it always ended with the same image—Maria Ema running after the Baptistas, losing her hat in the dust, trotting along the broad road with her braids unraveling. Calling out to the people in the cart to help her, when she was just eighteen.

Then, with her back to the chair on which Walter's daughter was sitting, Alexandrina would vent her anger. Yes, even then she still felt disgusted. No one had realized the Baptistas had kept their eldest daughters in and left Maria Ema to run wild, that they had allowed their youngest daughter to approach the buggy. She, her own mother, Baptista's wife, was to blame. When it comes to trouble with sex, the mother is always to blame, however she may protest. She had let him draw her daughter, capture her within the four edges of the white sheets on which he drew his portraits. And Walter had done not just one drawing but ten, possibly twenty. With a hat, without a hat, with braids, without braids, with clothes and without clothes, with flowers in her hair and without. And birds too. Part dove, part pigeon, part nightingale. Others had said—part hawk. The good-for-nothing. At that point, people started making bets, it was said that all the girls he used to draw had taken their clothes off for him. And, according to Alexandrina's biblical version, he must have drawn about ten or twelve, poor things, poor, poor things, all along the roads.

Yes, she had inherited all those stories long before the night of rain. They were not coarse stories. They simply were.

She had merely inherited the stories, just as they were. Walter was only marginally involved with that ballast of images. She knew that. Walter was just a passerby.

25.

But Francisco Dias was greatly aged by the shock of his son leaving for India when he should have been coming home to make good the harm done to the Baptistas. Because Maria Ema's father and mother were beginning to torture her. While they shut themselves up in the house, bowed by the weight of the dishonor, they forced their daughter to do all the shopping, to carry heavy weights, to run errands to places where they knew there would be lots of people to see her, they exposed her to general view by making her sit at the window, by the rose tree, on Sundays and on Saturday afternoons, so that her suffering would be complete, and when she was not broken by that, they had locked her in her room, opening the door just a crack to give her some food and then immediately bolting it again. So people said. And Francisco Dias, who considered himself to be a man of honor and compassion, had written a letter to Walter telling him how her parents were torturing her and telling him to come back soon on leave to make reparation.

He had written four letters, one after the other, each one shorter and more urgent, describing Maria Ema running after the cart, the scene that had made his sister Adelina cry so much. On the fifth letter he had only got as far as writing the place and the date. As he was writing the first line, Francisco Dias set down his pen on the desk where he did the farm accounts and decided to go in person to find his son, in that barracks marooned in the middle of an infinite plain and of which he had so often dreamed. He put on some calf-leather boots and spent one night and a whole morning on a hard train seat in order to see his son. But instead of his son, he saw a commandant who had him sit down in an armchair and who didn't even bother to call in Walter Glória Dias, no longer Private Dias, but Corporal. Hard though it was to believe, during training, Walter Dias had been the best at tracking, fencing, scrambling over walls, and at sticking swords into straw dummies. He was also the best shot, the fastest soldier on marches and crossing swamps; he had been the first to drive the commandant's car and the first to step forward when asked, during training, who was prepared to go and defend Portugal's power in India. Corporal Walter Dias had enlisted to leave for Goa.

Francisco Dias, however, had not lost two days' work at home in order to learn of such commitments, but to explain about a pregnant girl, about a shameful affair which had its roots in Walter's very nature. But the commandant was in cahoots with the corporal. He too was a man of few words—"Well, let him decide then." And after a long, long wait, Walter had appeared at the door to decide whether he preferred to do the decent thing by Maria Ema or to go and serve in India, but he had said nothing. The commandant, though, made the decision for him. He said it would be very difficult to prove Walter was the father, that Francisco Dias should consider carefully, he might be ruining his own son's future. Francisco Dias got to his feet. No, he wouldn't do that, things would work out, and he was the last person to want Walter back. Thus his youngest son would set off, whistling, on board the steamship *Pátria*. His globe-trotting son Walter. That was what his father said.

26.

The niece could hear if she wanted to, and if she didn't want to, then she shouldn't listen. The globe-trotter would not come back to Valmares before leaving for India. The globe-trotter had found a patron. He had probably started drawing the moment he arrived at the barracks. He had probably drawn thousands of those human-eyed birds touching beaks, or thousands of bird-encircled human figures touching mouths. He knew the son God had given him. He did not believe Walter was the best at fencing, the best at fighting, the best at tracking and at performing somersaults. He believed that it was his skill at drawing that lay behind the recognition which was translated into the strip of cloth that had turned him into a corporal. There was something else going on too, perhaps, something subversive. Walter's mysterious rise, in a place where he had been sent to be punished and when he should have been thinking about what to say to the Baptistas, made Francisco Dias suspect murky dealings.

And on certain winter nights, Francisco Dias—out loud and in front of those directly involved—would recall the moment when he had got off the train at Valmares station and had seen the roof of his own house in the distance and, as he approached, his son Custódio laboring in the courtyard. His submissive son, schooled in endurance by his childhood experience of polio. His son Custódio, always ready to defend Walter's behavior. He had gone into the house, sat down at the table and looked at his crippled son as he sat among his other sons. And it had suddenly come to him, as if a lamp had been lit behind his eyes: Custódio was the son he needed. He remembered that hour, that intelligent day, that brilliant moment. He had leaned across the table—"Custódio, you won't let me down, will you?" It was cold again on the narrow, barren plain. The bare almond trees seemed more like spiders' webs than trees. The fig trees were leaning earthward as if abandoned. And father and son, having reached an understanding, an agreement, put down their forks and napkins, hitched a horse to one of the carts and set off slowly, talking, in the direction of the road. Until they got to the Baptistas' door. Francisco Dias was in a cautious mood, but he felt he was acting both intelligently and honorably. It was true Walter was not sitting by his side as he should have been, as was only right, but in order to make up for the mistakes of his youngest, he had brought with him his oldest son. And then they knocked on the door and went in.

An hour later, Maria Ema left the house wearing a woolen jacket over her shoulders and carrying just one bag; and she stepped up into the cart, helped by Custódio Dias. Maria Ema received her husband early one Saturday morning, wearing a long velvet jacket trimmed with astrakhan and a felt hat with a white feather on it. But there is no record, no public memory of the event. It existed above all in Francisco Dias' evening conver-

sations, mostly with his friends, to show them what an intelligent man can do when confronted by unexpected difficulties.

And there was no reason why the distracted niece should
hear. But if she wanted to know, then let her, sitting with her
back to them as usual. But she knew.

27.

She knew too that Maria Ema would have waited for Walter,
because he had not been silent, he wrote, sent her drawings and
more drawings as he traveled on and with each new sighting
of land. He sent them from São Tomé, from Luanda, from
Lourenço Marques. He sent them to his dear father and his
dear brother en route to India. But it was not long before
everyone realized who they were intended for. Custódio always
knew. In 1947, communications took time, the months were
long, the evenings endless, journeys slow, slow enough to think
and then think some more, to imagine all kinds of things between going and coming, between what one said and what one
knew. Five facts were enough to fill a life. It was best that those
facts should be separated by water, love and letters. Longing
moored between the walls of the house. The years could pass,
though waiting was not always easy. She, nevertheless, waited.

Walter's daughter would find this out.

The proof is that Maria Ema would not share a bedroom
with Custódio Dias. Francisco Dias' eldest son would not

enter the room in which Maria Ema Baptista slept until after Walter's return from India, when Walter's daughter was three years old, when they had that photo taken together, on the day when the three of them escaped in the black buggy. The laborers thought it was Custódio himself who had helped them escape. He must have taken them to the station in the buggy. He must have set them free on that day in the summer of 1951. Custódio was already referred to cruelly as a cuckold. The cuckold must have wanted that photograph of the two of them to be taken, father and daughter in front of the camera. The cuckold must have protected them. It became known that, for a few hours, the three of them were a family. But the cuckold had the patience of thistles, the cuckold waited. They say that the cuckold knew in 1951, when the Valmares house was still crammed with various members of the Dias family, that the other man would run away and that they would all join forces to drive Walter out.

That's what they say, that, during that summer, Walter had driven the buggy as never before. Wearing his khaki uniform, he would leap onto the buggy and race off, wearing out the mare with his journeyings. Both cart and horse were nicknamed the Devil's Chariot. The women would lock up their daughters, and the girls, captive, silent, docile as sheep, would stand at the windows to watch the quartermaster from India go by. In Valmares everyone expected the worst, apart from Custódio who, as he always had, watched for his return. "Let him go. People have to do what they have to do"—Custódio would say. Only later, months after Walter had set sail on the

High Monarch to Melbourne, did Maria Ema open her bedroom door to Custódio Dias, and only then did he begin to father her children.

That was after his departure for Lisbon, London, Melbourne.

According to the brothers who took him to the station at Valmares, Walter had started his journey in a linen suit. In Blé's version, that suit cost him very dear later on. It didn't matter what they said, that was how his daughter imagined him, traveling from port to port: very erect, in a light-colored suit, and a gold watch on his left wrist. If he had not come back in 1963, that is how his daughter would have inherited him.

28.

But she used to follow Custódio Dias around too. She appreciated the fact that Maria Ema's husband kept silent about his own life. She was fascinated by the slow, cautious asymmetric steps he took around the house. She used to follow him out into the courtyard, down the narrow paths, into the adjoining huts where the smaller animals were kept and the stables where the horses flicked their tails. Sometimes, Custódio would go to the old storehouse where he would dump anything that was no longer wanted. The storehouse was separated from the house by a carpet of straw and mud. In this tumbledown place slept the runt of the chicks and the chicken that could no longer lay and that had a bell tied to its leg. Rusty hooks found shelter there, as well as piles of rickety tables, cracked vases, the leather collars of dead mules. It was known as the junk room and that was where the black buggy was stored in the unbearable summer of 1955. The daughter saw in its buckled base a living being waiting to move. It may have been covered in dust, but that had been Walter's cart. Her legs shook when she walked away from it.

But in the autumn of that year, she was already leaping over the shafts of the carriage and driving it fearlessly, because during the day the countryside was bright and at night it was dark, but she still had the revolver in her bedroom, and in the junk room, as everywhere else, Walter's daughter was safe, for she was accompanied by solitude. Though still small, with no waist and no figure, she would urge on a nonexistent mare, ride along tarmac roads she had never known and, under cover of the darkness of the junk room, she carried grasped beneath her arm Walter's cartridge paper, his Viarco paints and his Faber pencils. But because she was holding the bits of string that restrained the racing, absent mare, she did not draw any birds; instead, sitting between the shafts, she would roar out the names of the birds she did not draw. The autumn was as clear-skied as summer. The sun would go into hiding, leaving a single horizontal ray between the hills and the clouds. Francisco Dias approached in his hobnail boots. He stopped at the door of the junk room. While the Dias brothers withdrew into the house, he would yell—"Someone's got into the junk room, they're on that buggy. Get whoever's in there out..." The dark winter of 1956.

"What's my daughter-in-law's child doing on that buggy?"—he bawled, standing at the broad junk-room door, in the dead of night, in late spring. "Get her out of there!"—he said to Blé the foreman. "Get her out of there once and for all!" Francisco Dias did not realize that even if they did get her out of there, she would still be there, and he wouldn't understand that to the day he died. He was one of those people oblivious to the gap that exists between action and being, a gap that no one bridges and which transforms each man into human matter. Unaware of that, he would ask—"Isn't the child afraid?"—as Blé removed her, shooing her away as he did the chickens. "Why isn't she afraid?"

No, inside the junk room, she wasn't afraid. As she stood firmly on the deck of the buggy, reins in her hand, the old hulk became an amphibious vehicle, a carriage, a long train, a giant steamship crossing the seas. Still so small, with no waist, no breasts, without even her second teeth, Walter's daughter stood at the helm looking out at the meadows undulating with wheat, slicing through mud and waves, conquering the winds and the damp of the seas, the glow of evening on the water, the pitch-black night falling on all the oceans she had ever heard of. Walter's daughter was not afraid. That was what troubled Francisco Dias and the Dias brothers who had not yet left in 1957. They were not frightened of her, but of the fact that she wasn't afraid of the dark on nights when the Moon hid her white face from the Earth.

It troubled them that their niece did not need any light to go up to her room, that she went up the stairs and went to bed without even lighting a match. Even Maria Ema was troubled by this. João Dias and Inácio Dias, who had not yet left for America, would come back to the table saying they had found her in the corridor, in the dark, slipping fearlessly past the large plant pots, as if she were an old lady, and she wasn't even a proper person yet. Maria Ema also found it odd that Walter's niece wasn't afraid, and that was why she would put on a light for her. She would force her to keep a light burning, to watch the oil burning out in the lamp by her head, so that she could go down to her husband, her father-in-law, to her brothers- and sisters-in-law and tell them everything was normal. She herself lit the light so that the child would not be afraid of a fear she did not even have, and Custódio Dias would ask as he was laying the fire—"Wasn't our daughter afraid?" Maria Ema would bend over the table, burying her face in the things she was sewing. She was always sewing. "We're all afraid of something, aren't we?" The mild winter of 1957.

But Custódio Dias had a different way of removing his niece from the buggy. He would approach from the porch, with his consistently irregular step, take his flashlight out of his pocket, and, not realizing how far the beam of his flashlight reached, he would light up the route of the *High Monarch* across the sea. He could probably see the water too. With his flash-light on, Custódio would approach slowly, reach out his arms and lift her down from between the shafts, take her hand and lead her back to the house. Kindness existed, it took on human form and sometimes merged with the body of Custódio Dias. He silently led her back to the house. Only he knew how the niece had come to inherit Walter's buggy.

29.

By 1958, though, Custódio was leading her back to a house in which there were only two windows lit. The Dias brothers had left for good. The sly creatures had gone. And she would learn that slyness is not the same as lying, it is not a strategy or a plan, it is an instinct, what remains of an animal with a quick grasp, and which sleeps out the time of waiting, coiled up safe in the soul, as if asleep. Except that it isn't asleep. A part of it watches and acts from afar, not out of a spirit of good or evil, but simply out of instinct. A kind of vengeance savored beforehand, lingeringly, tenaciously, sleepily, with the eyes open, then closed. Waiting. The product of some gland perhaps. For slyness cannot be learned, it is born, it emerges, like red hair on the body or a widow's peak, which merely mark a person out, classify them, but no more than that. So it is with slyness. With the departure of the Dias brothers, she inherited a knowledge of that particular human type, of that uncatalogued form, existing alongside mammals and birds. There's something about the face of a sly person, their lips, their eyes, a kind of intelligence that colludes with the death that exists in time. That was how the Dias brothers were. Perhaps they still remembered a morning spent battling against dung, a memory that lay curled and waiting in their lives, waiting to leave. An affront that had gradually eaten away at them from the inside.

The Dias brothers had begun to leave two years after Walter, giving only a week's notice. She remembered Adelina and her husband, Fernandes, the one who had studied Electricity and who had taught her the letter W for Watt and for Walter. She remembered Joaquim, Manuel and their respective wives. Perhaps their sons and daughters. Of Luís, João and Inácio, all bachelors, she had a clearer memory of their names and ages than she did of their faces, but as a whole, she recalled them as being utterly submissive to their father, impotent, obedient as trained mules, and yet, meanwhile, they had been plotting among themselves, working on their plan to leave Valmares, saying nothing out loud, but muttering in corners, their wives keeping their lips tight shut. When her father asked what they were talking about, Adelina Dias would say—"Oh, nothing, Pa!" And they all followed the same pattern. They started to spend Sunday evenings out of the house, then Wednesday nights, then other nights. They would go off and come home late, and, as if everything were conspiring in that plot born of natural slyness, not even the guard dogs would bark when they came in. Their father appointed spies, but the spies were already in on the plot. It was Adelina's husband, Fernandes, who began the process, and the others followed in his footsteps. Francisco Dias' sons used to go into São Sebastião to study foreign words from a dictionary and a Teach Yourself book. When they returned home late, they would slip stealthily in through the side door, with bits of paper stuffed in their pants pockets. She saw them one by one, coming in through the courtyard, being insulted by Francisco Dias, who had grown thin and confused—"You scum, you bastards!" And they said nothing.

Besides, they did not really exist for Francisco Dias. Only as they announced their departure did they gain some singularity in the house and take on a degree of individual identity for their father; they emerged from the bundle, from the production line, from the brigade of workers they had been to become identifiable people. To be called up one by one before the suitcases they would pack at night. Unlike the other farm workers who celebrated such departures with a party that was part wake and part fanfare, the Dias brothers left without a word, without warning. They left the tools, the animals, the dung, the fields, the women, the children and the big rooms, without a word, as if they were going off on the train to do some shopping and would be back the next day. They promised they would soon return. They did not tell Francisco Dias where they were going. They used to lie. She remembered. She had inherited that image of pure slyness. The Dias brothers broke free from their father like rabbits. Silent and swift as hares in dreams. They broke free.

30.

On that rainy night, she could see Francisco Dias' sons turning their backs on the wheat, on the threshing machines, on the fields, on the day laborers, turning their backs on the world of the Valmares fields, and delivering themselves over to steam-ships, photographs of which helped to feed her idea of the *High Monarch*, the British ship that had borne Walter away. She could imagine them taking their freedom silently and conspir-atorially, only letting out bold cries once they were actually at sea. Fernandes and Joaquim were the first to leave in 1953, then Manuel and Luís in 1954, João in 1956, and Inácio in 1957. Moving off, disappearing, vanishing miraculously into the dis-tance, all mixed up together, plunging into strange, arduous jobs, sending later for wives and children, never to return, prov-ing themselves fiercer and harder than Francisco Dias, out-doing even Walter. And bringing Walter back.

Yes, it is vital that Walter should realize tonight how his daughter inherited the emptiness in the house in Valmares, the immense doors, the transoms above the doors that let in the light and that reflected the passage of footsteps. The silence of the empty house, the echo of every room, of the corridors linking them, of the dark wooden floors. How she had inher-ited that silent, expectant space, the attic room in the midst of the other rooms, how she had inherited dominion over the labyrinth, the burgeoning emptiness between the walls, the checkered shadows, the repetition of the doors, their symme-try, all the spaces where the brothers no longer were, and how, with their departure, everything had been filled with Walter's presence.

It was the same for Francisco Dias. Walter came back, but differently this time. Francisco Dias would angrily remove his hat—"They all followed in his tracks, he's the one who got them all stirred up with that story he told them about money when he was here in '51. He set the trend. He's the one who pushed them out. Him!" And Francisco Dias tried to do all the work himself; he barely slept, he would get up at four in the morning, waking Alexandrina and Blé as well, and, even before the stars had faded, he would be standing outside the house shouting—"Custódio, come here!"—with all his work force taken from him. But they were healthy yells. They were proof of Walter's far-off resilience. Wherever Walter might be, he would be sitting with his back turned to it all. He would be fine.

31.

Yes, she was sure of that. Maria Ema had lacked staying power. She had allowed Walter's army kit to crumble into dust. Maria Ema had lacked the ability to wait, lacked the necessary coherence, hardness and fixity to wait for Walter, unlike his niece. Because, more and more, she was his niece. Not that it mattered. However silent Custódio Dias was, however often he took her on his lap or sat her on his knees in the cart, she was waiting for the other one, unlike Maria Ema, who had not waited. Then, in 1953, Maria Ema had stood for a moment in the doorway, against the light, and the niece noticed a bulge on her body. A bulge a bit like a bag. Maria Ema had some sort of bag attached to her female body. The niece hadn't seen this before and she didn't understand what had made Maria Ema's body grow and become misshapen, but even though she was unable to decipher the mystery, she understood that Maria

Ema had given in to Custódio. And then, one after the other, came three full bags, three children that looked like him and like her. She wore a pleated smock and a skirt with an elastic waistband. And why?

Because Custódio took her in the carriage to Faro, to the cinema to see Charles Boyer, and left her to dance with her cousins and sisters at the social club, while he hung around by the buffet. Because he bought her a sable jacket which she wore only twice a year, and which some years she didn't even put on. He took her to the hairdresser's, brought her nylons, lacquered furniture, a heater, a Luxor radio, a Swedish machine she could dance to in the evenings, and magazines in which you were asked to identify with either Michèle Morgan, Vivien Leigh or Ava Gardner and the results of which were supposed to tell you a woman's character. And Custódio did all this against his father's wishes, against his father's frugality, against that whole family enterprise, whose guiding principle had always been to spend only the absolute minimum. Francisco Dias quarreled with Custódio Dias, then made peace. After all, he was increasing the family with new grandchildren, just when the other sons and grandsons were leaving for Canada, the United States and South America. As if they were determined to scatter themselves around the world, as if they wanted to create the very opposite of Francisco Dias' united states. It was as if, year after year, the family table were breaking into splinters, with each splinter going off to another part of the world. Then toward the end of 1958, Francisco Dias gave in to Custódio Dias' extravagant regime. There was only one son now in the vast house in Valmares, but Francisco Dias still expected the others to return. Francisco Dias walked across the fields worked by strangers and blessed the hour God had given him a lame son, because he would never leave, he would wait there humbly for the others to come back. And spitting on the earth, he thought with bitterness, with deep dislike, with real rage about Walter Dias, the wanderer, the harbinger of that domestic diaspora. The image of the cockpit in which the two foreigners had died, almost in his own backyard, and the secret hope he had nurtured then, brought back to him the idea that a man dreams of things God scorns to dream about. Time itself seemed to him false and scornful. And night fell.

32.

The calm, extraordinarily sad nights of the peaceful year of 1959. When the doors were closed for the night, there were only three adults in the house. And Francisco Dias wanted to know where the wanderer, the voyager, the traveler had sent this year's Christmas card from. The son about whom no one could say he's this or that because he was and wasn't so many things. This year he sent some birds resembling thrushes from Florida. Was Florida in America? And what about Canada? Had he left Canada and the Bay of Fundy where he ate raw fish?

From there he sent silver-collared kingfishers diving for fish. The money he spent over there on colored pencils would be enough to buy up all the entailed estates for sale around Valmares. Now the wanderer was moving down the globe. He was in the West Indies. Doing what in the West Indies? Whatever he was doing, in his spare time he was painting yellow birds which he said were the size of flies. He didn't have any spare time, all he did was draw and paint. That wasn't possible, he must do something to raise money in order to set sail again. We must not forget that some people work on ships. Francisco Dias shuddered. His son working on a ship! The miserable globe-trotting wretch. But it wasn't true. The following day, they received a letter containing a drawing of an eagle—"He must be on dry land, because he's drawing eagles."

Where had he sent the eagles from? From India, during his stay there? No, from India he had sent mostly peacocks and crows. He had sent eagles from Angola. No, from Brazil. No one knew anymore. But Maria Ema knew, although she didn't say, or only if Custódio asked. This time she knew. He sent parrots from Brazil, pintail ducks from Panama, storks from Casablanca, hummingbirds from Caracas. Oh yes, she knew. Custódio showed his father how much she knew. Francisco Dias would get angry. It wasn't right that his daughter-in-law, the legal wife of Custódio Dias, should know so much about her brother-in-law's whereabouts. There was no need to memorize the stamps on the letters containing the drawings of birds, because for Francisco Dias birds were pretty much the same all over. And Walter, the wanderer, instead of sending photographs and postcards as his other sons did, sent drawings of birds. Nothing but feathers. Did the wanderer know anything apart from how to draw feathers? He left in his wake a rain of feathers. He pitied anyone fool enough to go after him. Maria

Ema, sitting hunched between Custódio Dias and Francisco Dias, remained silent. Her daughter knew all this, long before Walter visited her that rainy night.

33.

She also knew how, for five years, Francisco Dias had waited for his sons' return, and how, little by little, without giving even the slightest sign, he had begun to live an El Dorado of waiting that bore no relation to reality. In the magnificently empty house, where one only heard the occasional footstep, he would imagine the imminent collective return, vivid, absent presences, flesh-and-blood people, who moved about in a sea of bolivars and dollars.

Money, a river of money flowed about the feet of each of those sons, and all those rivers were, as one, sliding and snaking, month after month, toward Valmares. He didn't care about the furrow in the snow into which, far far away, one of his sons repeatedly plunged while trying to load logs onto a truck he couldn't keep up with—*Here they do their best to kill us and yet they pay us almost nothing*—Nova Scotia—wrote one of them, Luís Dias. He wasn't even worried about the dark mine beneath some lakes where Manuel worked for months on end, never seeing the light of day, because, as Manuel himself said, he didn't really exist below- or above-ground. The photograph showed him wearing a metal hat with a light attached to it and carrying a bucket in his hand, his face gleaming with sweat. Nor did he care that another son might get buried beneath the wooden houses he was demolishing with a pickax. He wasn't interested in a landscape so vast one could easily lose in it the plump dairy cows that Francisco Dias detested. Nor could he imagine what another son could be doing in the hills of Caracas, a son who described how he had refused to deliver bread from door to door like the postman in Valmares. He also listened to Custódio reading out the letters about the harsh, endless work on a railway, along which his son-in-law struggled, making his way ever farther west. There was even a letter, addressed to Adelina, that bore a bloody fingerprint. It said something like—*Forgive me, Adelina, I didn't want to send you this letter, but I haven't got any more paper or ink here, and I need to send you news of me today. I don't know what else to do, my fingers are worn down almost to the quick...*Nor did he want to know about the wives who had followed them, along with their children, and who now lived apart from them in small wooden rooms. He didn't want to know. Besides, the Dias brothers wrote little and were reticent when talking about their lives. But the paucity of details only fortified Francisco Dias' imagination. He knew more or less where they were, and he did not want to go any deeper into what he did know, for it all seemed to him part of an interpolated narrative about an interpolated world whose meaning would only be fully revealed when they returned. Otherwise, it had nothing to do with him.

It was as if his sons and his son-in-law had to go through an initiation ceremony whose stages were obscure and painful but necessary, and the details of which he did not wish to know, he just wanted it to be over. He wanted his children to reach the end and tell him they were millionaires. He could see them coming back, as surely as the ticking of the living room clock, to manage the quantities of money flowing toward his house like water from a spring. He wasn't interested in the lives or deaths of individual members of the Dias family. He wasn't interested in the before and after. "Before" was just his father who had left him the house, and "after" was the fortune his indistinguishable sons would bring to it. Nothing before, nothing after, nothing far away and nothing internal. He was interested only in the horizons of his own land, his familiar god to whom he dedicated the discipline of his will. Honor, love and life could only be justified if transformed into hectares of land. I recall that time in which he lived in a state of euphoria, against the grain of events, while his granddaughter stumbled over the syllables of ancient languages in the superstitious belief that one day they would become modern again. For five years, they were bound together by the same space and separated by contrary hopes. I remember that time tonight, so that Walter will know.

Francisco Dias even went so far as to ask landowners who were in a hurry to get rid of their farms and scrubland to wait for the first of his sons to come home. Adelina and her hardworking husband, as well as all the others, would be arriving at any moment. He believed that. He would get up in the middle of the night and order Alexandrina to clean the house in preparation. And yet, the next day, they were still not back. Even the day laborers were on the move, crossing the border into Europe, driven by poverty, and those who stayed, finding themselves indispensable, asked for more money, Francisco Dias began to leave land fallow, he stopped pruning the fig trees and closed up the hives, while he waited for his sons. Whenever a family took off, leaving the house to crumble and the fields to succumb to nettles, he would imagine buying what they abandoned in order to level and plant it. He would walk across the uncultivated fields and past the roofless houses nearby as if he already owned it all. He would end up with everything, he would be lord of all that abundance of land. He had only to wait. For him, something was happening that would prove more important than the invention of the wheel. A great hope prowled Valmares. The two of us were separated by our different ideas of the future and by the table at which we ate. We did not exchange a single word, nor did we understand each other. I thought the Dias brothers would never come back, while Francisco Dias could already hear their footsteps outside the house. Soon they would be back, and they would all come home rich, except one. "Except one, except one!"–he would shout, getting up from the table. Because Walter would not come back.

And suddenly, in the summer of 1962, a letter from Walter arrived. He sent various drawings of birds from cold climates, loons from the north, flying over the surface of some sea, and in the body of the letter written in a clear hand, taking up the whole page, he said something so extraordinary it had to be read out several times. Walter Dias wrote that he intended to come home.

34.

What kind of letter was that?

Francisco Dias had to lean on the table to steady himself. It wasn't possible. The wanderer would never return. The true vocation of a wanderer was not to return to the starting place, unless he was unable to wander the world anymore and was forced to stay in a place which reminded him of where he had come from. Unless he was ill or at death's door, the wanderer would never return home. We could sleep easy, Francisco Dias would say. His son Walter was thirty-eight, at the peak of his wandering career, he wouldn't come. But if he did, if that chanced to happen, it would be in order to engender something strange and possibly dark, at a time when the house in Valmares, the domain of Custódio Dias' irregular footsteps, most needed peace, until the others came back. No, he wouldn't come. And to make sure he didn't, to ensure that such an idea never even crossed his mind, a closely argued letter should be dispatched at once, dissuading him from coming. And what would that letter be like? Francisco Dias smiled.

It would be a letter couched in the most sombre of terms, a letter which he himself would write. A black letter, dissuading him from any return, for the wanderer had been to far too many places, unlike his brothers who had settled in safe, rich regions. He would have to be explicit. He couldn't come back. Walter was used to rapid modes of transport, steamships, planes, long-distance trains, he no longer knew how to be still or to walk along at his own pace or to obey the slow steps of an animal. In the house in Valmares, there were only slow modes of transport, muleteers on dirt tracks with steep verges, winding through meadows. The transport available was of the most utilitarian and practical kind, the cheapest too. For that reason, he should not come.

The hoods on the carts had been removed and now lay on the ground where Alexandrina's chickens used them to lay their eggs in. Like large nests. The chassis were still used to transport goods, straw, tools, whatever was needed to make the soil fertile, something that was becoming more and more difficult. Who could imagine Walter Dias coming all that way to climb onto the carcass of an old cart? Then there was the carriage. It was still in good condition, cleaned and cared for by Blé, but the truth was the pair of beasts that pulled it were too unevenly balanced now and it took all Custódio's patience to drive it. Could anyone imagine Walter Dias driving a carriage pulled by such a pair of horses? No one there could. Francisco Dias was talking out loud now. The buggy wouldn't do, either. It had been relegated to the junk room, the hood removed and hung from the roof, and the fabric had changed from white to black. The cobwebs and the dust had transformed it into little more than an old barrel that would be burned on a bonfire next winter to warm the two remaining day laborers. Not that he should expect to find them there either. If he was thinking of coming back and still hoping to be able to use the black buggy, he should know that the two mares that used to pull it had long since disappeared. None of that existed anymore. So what would the wanderer have to do at home?—asked Francisco

Dias, writing his son's real name on the paper, rather than that disrespectful nickname.

But when he reached the end of the letter, he paused before signing it. He reread it. His hand trembled. It was as if he had just revealed to himself the true state of his own land, signed by him in ink on paper.

Was what he had just written true? Had his house, his enterprise, his image of a frugal, productive empire been reduced to that state of decay? Why were his emigrant sons taking so long to come back? Why did they not write, or write just a few words on the back of postcards? Why did they behave like traitors? Francisco Dias realized that, for the first time and without anyone asking him to, he had just set down the harsh reality of his own life. It took him a while to finish the letter, but he finished it as it should be finished—"In other words, son, don't come home."

35.

He would come, he was longing to come home, Walter said in the brief letter that crossed with Francisco's. Brief enough to leave room on the paper for a drawing of a bird. A creature from a cold climate. The letter left no room for doubt. The wanderer wanted to return.

He was coming back. But Francisco Dias didn't understand why. And, if he did come back, why didn't Walter stay at a boardinghouse near the sea, why was he coming home when there was no room at the house in Valmares? The eighteen-room house was crammed with remnants, with emptinesses, with missing objects, it was full of absences and departures. There wasn't room for the impending visitor. Had it been another son who was coming back, everything would have been different, he would have been made welcome, the rooms were there waiting, that was the only reason they were kept clean and tidy, but it was the unwanted son who was coming back. In short, in a house crammed with all those who had left, there was no room for Walter.

Tall, thin, bent, his neck so stiff he had to turn his whole body in order to look to the side, Francisco Dias walked up and down the corridor several times, banging on each door with his stick. There were over thirty doors in the house, but none of them he felt should be opened to his son Walter. Far away, in the place from which he had sent that bird, that was where he belonged. He knew, he sensed that the bird of passage would not be the bringer of good news, that he would destroy the harmony between the couple who sustained the house, come between Custódio and Ema, upset his father, excite his three small nephews and confuse his niece, who was now nearly a young woman. "No, don't come!" But Custódio intervened. Custódio had the courage of those who have lost everything even before the battle begins, and he loved his brother, the brother who had everything he lacked. It was as if his other half were on his way to meet him. He couldn't wait to have Walter back. And it was agreed he would come back soon. According to his letters, which got shorter and shorter, and were always signed with a bird, the wanderer would arrive on the evening of the twenty-second of January 1963.

36.

It was December 1962. That year and that month are contained inside this night, so that Walter will know how Maria Ema reacted. She is the one I see most clearly.

The mother of Walter's nephews changed from one moment to the next. Without saying a word about her brother-in-law's visit, she would walk about on tiptoe and stop dead whenever Francisco Dias read out loud to Custódio in a booming voice the letters he wrote to Walter—"Don't come home, don't come home!" Then there would be another argument. It was inconceivable that Francisco Dias should want to close the door in a visiting son's face. Maria Ema would walk noiselessly to the end of the corridor, rest her head on the bundle of sheets in her arms, then look up again in the direction of the carob trees set in the ground like ships with green sails. Those ships with evergreen leaves, flourishing in the December earth, were moving off at invisible speed like primitive animals that might just speak to her. Maria Ema saw this. She raised her head from the sheets, placed the sheets in the basket, walked back down the corridor, stopped again, and jumped as if some shadow living in the house had suddenly moved and grabbed her from behind. She shuddered and hunched up her shoulders, hiding her face. She was listening. Through the dining room door, Francisco Dias was reading again—"Don't come home, don't come home, Walter!" The argument was continuing. Maria Ema ran the whole length of the house. She went from window to window, from end to end, of the quadrangular house. She came and went very seriously, as if she were busy doing something very serious. But she wasn't doing anything. Sometimes, in a burst of energy, she would check the handles on the doors, turning them, testing their resistance. She advanced through the jungle of doors. Indeed, the whole house smelled of lavender and of change. Maria Ema had never moved so many objects around for any other Christmas. However, when Custódio Dias limped in through the door, she stopped whatever change she was making. She stood there holding the towels or the china, Alexandrina's name still unspoken on her lips. Alexandrina was helping. She too stopped. Maria Ema came to. Her life and her soul were unfolded before everyone as clearly as a map. Blé said to the remaining laborers—"It's soldier Walter's Christmas this year." It was a Christmas that would only happen at the end of January. And so it was. I recall the Christmas Day of 1962 on which Maria Ema wore a silk dress.

I remember the cold wind that day and the image of Maria Ema in her silk dress, a summer dress, standing in front of the mirror. Her sons are playing outside, waiting for her. The wooden cart is ready. And she is on the landing, looking somewhere beyond the mirror. Custódio is standing behind her, watching, and he too can see her somewhere beyond the mirror. Spread out on the bed, like someone waiting for someone else, arms wide, lies that sable jacket more suited to northern climes.

Suddenly, the mules stop, the bells seem not to exist. The room is filled with a glassy silence. Neither of them speaks. She is the prisoner of a daydream which is reflected in the mirror, she is standing before that reflected image, waiting. Alone, in silence, she waits. There is no grammar book from which one can learn the declension of this silent tragedy. Then, Custódio goes toward her, toward Maria Ema's bare shoulders, and says how cold it is. He goes further, he says it's still early, that Walter will not have set off yet. He would have if he were coming by ship, but he's coming by plane. He won't even have packed his suitcase, he'll do that on the eve of his departure, which, if his letters are to be believed, will only be in twenty days' time. "Not yet"–he says. "Not yet?" Standing in front of the mirror, Maria Ema returns, although she does not reveal how far she has traveled. Only then does she take off the dress. She stands there in nylon stockings, garters above the knee, satin slip, her back and shoulders bare. Her hair is disheveled. Maria Ema picks up the dress and, quite undramatically, as if her hands were the blades of sharp scissors, she holds it by the seams at the neck and tears it. Her face white, her eyes staring, the dress ripped open. The dress in shreds in front of the mirror. Maria Ema went over to the bed and curled up in it, on the wooden frame, under the blankets, as if that frame and those folds were her sole home, and only after several days did she reemerge.

In eight days' time, in three days, in two days. Just like the countdown to *Sputnik*. Just so that, tonight, Walter will know.

37.

From a distance, the time which was about to begin seems a mere interval, a brief scene that takes place between one door that opens in the East and another that closes in the West, and between those two curtains there is a whisper, a tumult, a bustle, as if the cold winter sand were boiling, as if a wind were blowing from inland, snatching at dresses, at the tails of coats and at umbrellas. And as if all this had happened on a single day, in a single hour. Silence before and silence afterward. As if that time had been dug out of the century in order to condense life. Because everything that happened had that time as its aim, and everything that came afterward flowed out of it like a response to the turmoil, the firecracker, the combustion that took place inside the house and reverberated amidst the vegetation and among the swift clouds passing overhead like the breasts of plump pigeons flying in from the sea. They came from the waves, they passed the cliffs, advanced over the grasslands on their way to unleash their sudden floods upon the steep hills. It was hard to say if that blessing occurred because of her waiting. Maria Ema's waiting.

The day of waiting.

Maria Ema was in her thirties, in the full splendor of life. She wore her hair with the edges rolled, a style she had seen in magazine pictures of Ingrid Bergman. The roll started at her temples and continued to her shoulders. She was putting on makeup. She was doing this for two men. I know, I saw it, and I summon up that moment. Custódio was by her side again and he himself handed her the makeup. She knew. There was an air about him of long-resolved despair, which explained that magnanimity. He walked across the floorboards and handed her the bag.

But Maria Ema's makeup consisted of just a touch of lipstick. That was all. The transformation lay in her mouth. Her white flesh grew paler next to the bright rose of her mouth. Maria Ema's mouth became a real rose, a brilliant, pearly rose, that put a sparkle in her eyes, smoothed her hair, made her waist more slender, her foot slimmer, her ankle finer, her hands softer. Applying the lipstick to her mouth revealed the whole of her. It was inexplicable how that happened. She, however, only applied it on important occasions and when she went to mass. Now she was painting her lips in front of the mirror, the same mirror where, three weeks before, she had torn a silk dress. But that piece of clothing, far more intimate than any dress, had been mended now and darned. She was in front of the mirror, wearing another dress, in blue wool, painting her mouth pink, a touch of orange and a touch of cinnamon, a tinge of red. And mother-of-pearl, as was the fashion then. She drew in her lips, pressing them together, then pushed them out again, drawing them tight, as she drew the lipstick across them for the tenth time, while outside the animals harnessed to the carriage pawed the ground. Custódio had bought new horses, spent nine *contos de réis* he shouldn't have spent, so that the horses were the same height. Walter's brother wanted Maria Ema to hurry up so that they could go and collect Walter, formerly soldier, then quartermaster, then traveler, and now who knew what Walter was. Custódio Dias himself had brought her the lipstick. Maria Ema was still retouching her lips. The difference between wearing makeup and not wearing it was as radical as being clothed and being naked. She, clearly, was naked.

How could a lame farmer cross the room and hand his wife the lipstick on the day she was waiting for his brother to arrive, if she was not naked? How could a man put his life and his love at risk, before his own brother, if part of her was not profoundly naked? And in Custódio's gesture there was passion, love, more than love, perhaps an imitation of perfection. Walter was not just coming from Australia, he was coming from Africa, from South Africa, from Tanzania, from Angola, from the coasts of South America and the Caribbean, from the West Indies, from the north, from North America, from the cold lands of Canada. He was dragging a piece of the world behind him, the soul of the world, a sense of movement through space. It was as if Custódio knew that for him there was no world, as if he had already lost forever everything he could lose and there was nothing left for him but giving, holding out the towel, handing over the lipstick. He gave it to her. She was applying the lipstick to her lips. She was getting up. Her hair carefully coiffed and her lips painted. It was hard for her to conceal her joy. Maria Ema resembled a tormented island that had risen to the surface and then sunk down again.

For eight days she had been submerged, now she rose up resplendent with her pearly pink lips. And then, just as she was putting the lipstick away, when we were all almost ready to go and fetch him and the horses were pawing the ground, Walter arrived. He arrived in a taxi.

38.

I can hear the wheels of the taxi and the taxi itself. Walter coming into the yard and the horses who had been restlessly pawing the ground startled into stillness. The taxi sliding gently over the mud, then over stone, the soft sound of tires approaching. In 1963, a taxi was still a rare sight. Inside the dark taxi was a man in a light raincoat, smoking a cigarette. First to emerge was the tail of his raincoat, then the hand holding the cigarette, immediately followed by the short hair and the whole body, but only then, when he looked at us, his feet firmly on the ground, did soldier Walter appear.

And he found us all at the door to greet him. We had no electricity, but we had a phone. Custódio had had one installed on the porch, for Maria Ema and their near neighbors. Walter had telephoned to say what train he would be on. But in Lisbon, he could not bear to wait for the train and had hired a taxi instead. And he had arrived when, imprisoned by the color of Maria Ema's lips, we were still not quite ready. Even she had not had time to put on her sable jacket or pick up her handbag. She hadn't adjusted her dress at the shoulders or put on her high heels. Custódio had not yet donned his brown overcoat. Francisco Dias was still without his hat or his sheepskin jacket. Walter's nephews had still not tied their shoelaces. Maria Ema's oldest child, that is, her daughter, had not finished arranging her ponytail. And it was in that hurried, incomplete state, with the horses still not harnessed to the carriage, the broom and the oilcan still leaning against the wheels, that Walter arrived. He arrived with his raincoat open and a dark blue suit on underneath, with two suitcases and a cigarette stubbed out on the ground. There he was before us, the seven of us surprised and standing to attention. And then we all embraced.

Walter enfolded Francisco Dias in a large embrace, cheek to cheek, chest to chest, hands on each other's back. Walter embraced his brother, cheek to cheek, their bodies pressed together. The same embrace, the same slaps on the back. Walter shook Maria Ema's hand, kissed her on both cheeks and called her sister—"My dear sister!" He lifted each of my brothers, his nephews, up to shoulder height and kissed the oldest girl, his niece, on both cheeks. He himself said—"Give your uncle a kiss!" He himself said that. They all did. They had agreed. They said—"Your Uncle Walter's here!" That's what she said. Maria Ema was barely twice the age of Walter's daughter and that is what she said. Maria Ema's joy made of her a reed in the wind. The wind, the breeze, life itself came from that newly arrived body, that dazzling body, known, foolishly, as soldier Walter. She herself shouted out—"Go on, off you go and open the door of your Uncle Walter's room!" It seemed impossible, but Walter Dias was there in body and soul, he was coming back, he had arrived.

39.

Walter Dias came in, took off his raincoat and sat down at the table; the fire was lit, and he rubbed his hands in front of it, shook his curly hair, kept his red scarf on over his dark blue suit, wiped the soles of his shoes on the mat at the door. He sat down at the table. He served himself from the tureen proffered by Alexandrina, he waited for them to speak, for them to ask him to speak. He was prepared for questions, but no one asked why Walter Dias had come back to his father's house. His presence spoke for him. He returned like one at ease in the space he lives in, a space he controls, fits, receives, adorns, values, empowers and explains. Walter was there and he did not need to explain why he had come, to give a reason for his arrival, he himself was the reason. Francisco Dias, sitting, as he always had, at the head of the table, accepted that too. Did anyone ask why soldier Walter had come back from abroad? No one. He himself said, with a deep sigh—"Well, here I am, brother!"—patting Custódio's hand, his sister-in-law sitting beside him. No one asked, not on that day or on the days that followed. And then it rained.

It rained. For several days it rained, the house was besieged by rain. It was as if the rain wanted the eight of us to sit there together around that table. Sometimes the rain was a deluge.

You could hear it beating on the roof tiles, the windowpanes, the closed doors, in the overflowing jugs, in the broken pots. It is January 1963 and we are, as I said, besieged by the rain. But however often I say it, it is not easy to drown out the noise of that furious water. It still dominates, suffocates, enters this moonlit night and transforms it, drenches it, fills it with liquid sounds. Tonight is suffused with the days following Walter's arrival in 1963. Later, it was said he had packed his blanket in one of his suitcases. I didn't see it, so I don't know. The cases were opened in the room that Alexandrina and Blé had tidied, whitewashed and polished. At the time, no one mentioned the blanket. Later, much later, they invented the presence of the blanket at that homecoming, but it doesn't matter. What matters is that the rain shut the eight of us up in this house. The clouds came from the waves, crossed the cliffs, progressed over the grasslands and unleashed their contents at the foot of the steep hills. The house was surrounded by rain, by the ponds, by the white lake into which the bean field had been transformed. We are surrounded by the squadrons of clouds that whistle over the roofs of the houses. The two day laborers are marooned beneath the porch, shifting from foot to foot in their hard, hobnail boots, like horseshoes. They too are the prisoners of the rain, prisoners of the weather, immediately outside, right next door to us, leaning against the walls, knowing that a different sort of man is inside the house, Walter. Everyone has seen Walter. No one asks what brings him there, what brings him back to Valmares, to his father's house. A different question is asked inside that sweet prison of rain. Maria

Ema asks it—"How much longer is this rain going to last?"—
Maria Ema standing with her back to us, lifting the curtains at
the window, and Walter going over to her to inspect the puffy
clouds, white, gray, Mediterranean. On the days immediately
after his arrival.

40.

Was it days, a week, two weeks of rain? Part of a day? The
night multiplies itself by nights, the day divides itself into several days of rain, falling between the sky and the bean field,
fine, hard, smooth, brilliant rain, falling in ropes, in threads, in
cascades, then suddenly clearing for a moment. But around the
table, by the crackling fire, day and night are one. The fire, the
table. The eight of us around the table. Why did Walter Dias
come back? What a pointless question to ask now.

He clears up the matter on the second day.

He came to explain to his father and his nephews and niece,
to his brother and his sister-in-law what life is like in Australia,
the shifting soil, the wooden houses, the far-flung farms, the
sandstorms, the inextinguishable forest fires, the coastline.
About his life in Canberra, in Sydney, in Melbourne. What the
people are like, what the parties are like. What India is like,
what Africa is like. Syntheses of syntheses formed from sights
and smells, the enchantment or disgust bears no resemblance
to what he wrote in his letters, it is all new again as he tells it,
as if he were once more forging a path around the world, feeling a boyish, adolescent joy that delights in the discovery of
each country's limits, of their differences and similarities. And,

finally, more syntheses. To his mind, India is too oily, everything gleams, even the sea with all its seaweed looks like olive oil. Australia is too far away, Africa too wild. Then the world began to change, to grow discordant. He knew because he had been in India. The violence was growing in Africa and it would be unstoppable, he foresaw catastrophes there. All peace-loving people should leave. The world is a big place, but there are always people who grow fond of a place. Not him, though. You can live quite happily anywhere, as long as you're free to leave for the next place. That way there will always be prosperity and peace. He prefers the Americas. His brothers were right to choose North America. He himself has just come from Ontario, where it's an entirely different world, where you can have a good life and live in peace. There a person can work and have time to do whatever he wants, he can earn enough money to travel and find time to draw. No, he doesn't sell his drawings, if someone likes one, he simply gives it away. Francisco Dias has his doubts, but he cannot come up with any counter-arguments. For the first time, he thinks that perhaps having a decent job is compatible with those drawings of birds.

41.

Yes, he talked about Valmares as well, but what he had to say was surprising. He abandoned the fire he was stoking to tell his brother and sister-in-law that they should get rid of the house and the land before it lost its value, and invest in a business on the coast. That it wasn't worth investing in mechanization on such scattered lands, separated by distance and by high stone walls. They should invest in the leisure industry before others got in on the act. Leisure was where the money would be. Leisure would be the next great source of wealth, the great engine of development and change in the world. Leisure would be a way of life, an aim, a cause. Someone had to invest in exploiting that cause.

But Francisco Dias distrusted those words. Leisure, to him, sounded too much like lazy and laziness and pleasure. How could leisure create money? Although leisure and laziness were quite different, how could such words be associated with assured profits? How could an industry depend on the desire of other people to do nothing? What if other people didn't want to do nothing? What if they wanted to work seven days a week as he had always done all his life? He wouldn't exchange a single one of his properties for the leisure industry. When had leisure ever produced any money? What kind of leisure could possibly be useful?—asked the wanderer's father of the person he called son, eyeing him distrustfully. But it isn't true that Walter pressed Francisco Dias, that he punished or threatened him, as people said. On the contrary.

Walter merely put his case more clearly. It was raining, we were still besieged, and he said that he had come to tell us that everything would change. That the change would not happen overnight, but that it would happen, it had already started, he knew. Walter Dias had come to tell us that it was time to move the Valmares house somewhere else. That we should flee what was about to happen as if from a storm or a fire. A white fire, a black tide that would leave us stranded in the middle of the plain. We had to sell the house, leave, move, take it somewhere else. And then Francisco Dias should have got angry, he should have shaken that image of the prodigal son, in front of his four grandchildren, but he did not want to respond, or did not need to, because he possessed a certainty, a trump card. His son Custódio had a problem with his foot, he would never leave. He would take care of everything until the others arrived.

I see Francisco Dias during that family conversation, that settling of accounts with the family business, that sacred act of the species. And the fact is that the father's eyes are laughing because Custódio's ankle is an anchor that keeps him tied there, by the grace of God who gave that illness to his eldest son, and gave Francisco a buoy for his boat, for his land and his house. Custódio's twisted foot is the salvation of his fortune, of his honor, of the honor of the remaining members of the Dias family. It is what binds us to the good old days, when Francisco Dias' house was a business, and to the good times soon to come. We can't go, we can't leave the land.

The land was the scattered land which, later, the other Dias brothers would accuse Walter of describing as an empire of stones and the house where we laid the fire and took shelter the crumbling headquarters of that empire of stones. A lie. I was the oldest of Walter's nephews and nieces. I heard everything Walter said, his words, his hesitations, his deep in-breaths, when he held in the smoke, the cigarette hovering near his lips.

I, who was his niece then, heard everything and I never heard him refer to Francisco Dias' house as an empire of stones. Perhaps the Dias brothers were confusing him with me, years later. *I* said that to them, I wrote to them saying it was a house of rotten walls and scrubland, an empire of stones. Maria Ema and Custódio lingered in that empire like two lizards wandering about in an abandoned Roman cistern. I wrote that too. But Walter never said it, he never offended them. That's a lie. He was just himself, not me. Not that it mattered.

42.

The wanderer, a much-traveled man, wore a dark blue suit and a woolen sweater, he made strange gestures and drew birds so that his little nephews could see, on the map, what the fauna and flora of the world he knew were like. He knew and he taught them. His niece, taller than his nephews, observed the drawings at a distance, on tiptoe, looking over her brothers' heads. She saw Walter getting the feel of the paper, shaking it, turning it around, then, taking up his pencil, making a rapid sketch with broad strokes, refining the details, concentrating on filling in the areas bordered by colored surfaces, his pencil moving up and down, the movement contained between his fingers. Sometimes they were quick sketches simply to illustrate the different species and the places where the birds lived, but other drawings were so vivid and alive, the faces so expressive, that the birds seemed to have souls. The children bent over the table for hours, watching as, from the sheet of paper, one bird emerged, then another and another and yet another, whole flocks of them escaping from Walter's fecund hand. Rapt and silent, while outside, the rain fell.

But suddenly, the drawings stopped, and Walter's nephews looked at Walter, not saying a word. Francisco Dias was stoking the fire, also not saying a word. Custódio Dias was looking at the drawings of birds and at the fire. And she came into the room too, she too was silent, she too struck an expectant pose, apparently casual, as if nothing was wrong. But it wasn't true. Walter's niece knew. When Maria Ema entered the room, she assumed a posture of defense and attack, of flight. The posture of one arriving. Everything about her was mobile, and since her head, topped by a ringlet, turned here and there, her breath, beneath the sound of the rain, provoked a seductive breeze in the house that mingled with the sound of the tea being poured and charged the sound with a new power, transforming it into a boiling cascade. Her hand trembled, the tea spilled, the cup handles collided with the wineglasses. Red stains appeared on the table. She said—"Oh!" The two brothers both rushed to help her. She laughed at both with the same painted mouth, but it was clear that Maria Ema had painted her lips for Walter alone. She was a woman in the prime of her youth, touched by visiting love, inflamed by the bonfire of desire, placed in extremis by the proximity of an embrace. Love, that being in the pink mask, placed a hand on her shoulder and pushed her in the direction of the human body where it had made its home. I can see her bent over the table, with the teapot in her hand, her face red, her legs trembling, her hair coming unpinned, I can see her stand up straight and run with the teapot over to the window and exclaim at the approach of the great thunder-bearing clouds. "Oh!"–she said again. Maria Ema's three youngest children ran to their mother's side, Custódio drew his children away from the window, he drew Maria Ema away from the coming thunder, holding her around the waist, removing her from the window. Francisco Dias was putting out the fire, Alexandrina was turning out the lights, Walter was calming everyone down. The lightning flash broke. He knew that in the Orient there were female typhoons and male typhoons, he knew about perilous currents, about storms that changed the course of rivers, he knew about natural catastrophes, the storms of Africa, the storms of the Indian Ocean, the cry of the halcyon warning of the approaching storm, the rains of Cabinda, the rains of Guinea, the thunderbolts of the equator that cut whole forests in two. Then, on the other hand, there were the clouds, the white storms of snow, the kidnapping of houses by a cold blanket of ice. Those clouds passing along the southwest coast of Europe, through that easy gate, where the weather merely grazes gently by, were nothing compared with nature's great upheavals, the hurricane in Florida, which he himself had never actually seen, but had heard described by someone who had, on his journeys through only a small part of the world. He still watched the birds though. Fugitive birds. And since Maria Ema was protected by Custódio's arms, she shrank back into them, in front of Walter. Walter Dias was there before her, before her and Custódio's children, his father and his daughter, whom everyone referred to as his niece, and before her husband, whom he called brother. But we were all right, we were in the dark of evening, corralled by the rain, by the passing thunder, easing, dispersing, returning, and starting again, as if it wanted to carry us all off forever, excited, perplexed, confused, wrapped in a sea of rain.

43.

Francisco Dias could not bring himself to ask why his youngest son had come back. The answer was there. He entirely filled the space he occupied, making everything around him essential. Crouched between the table and the fire, talking to the four children he called his nephews and niece, explaining, drawing birds he had never seen, but which he knew were hidden, sheltered in their holes, waiting for the storm to pass, so as to begin building their nests, he knew about the cuckoo, the redstart, the robin, the treecreeper, the bee-eater, the flycatcher, the nightingale, the golden oriole. As regards color, he knew where to find their light plumage, their dark feathers, their throats, heads, crowns, cheeks, faces, eyes, their long tail feathers. He was talking out loud—In order to draw a bird, any bird, you must start by drawing an egg. Inside the bird there is always an egg, that is its internal shape. After drawing the egg, you surround it with the least important part, the feathers. But you must take care with the feathers too, because they are what give the bird its beauty. You have to have a very steady hand to paint them. There is nothing harder than painting feathers. His nephews went off to fetch one; he separated out the barbs, put them back together again, showed them the flexibility and strength of the shaft, and then said—"Right now we'll copy it." But then he said that birds had thousands of feathers in layers, which we knew were there but couldn't see, that they formed smooth tufts, and if we half-closed our eyes, we would see a bird as if it were an arrangement of spots of color. "I'll do one like that!" And he picked up the charcoal and the eraser and gradually joined up the spots of color. He talked and the rain fell. I recall the rain and the end of the rain. "Draw another one, and another one, and now draw one flying!"

44.

When the storm passed, en route to the rest of Europe, the bean field was a lake of pools so deep they looked blue, the cold settled in and the frost made them glassy sheets. The sky was reflected in the glass and the water. Walter wrapped himself in his raincoat and made a phone call. He said he would pay the phone bill. That during those months he would pay for all such expenses. And he would phone, ask them to phone back, and wait. When he got a phone call, he would close the door. He seemed to be keeping something secret from everyone, preparing a surprise. He would laugh, Walter would laugh. He did not know what his brothers would say later about the triumph that made him laugh on the phone, but now he was laughing. He laughed a lot. Walter's laugh. His rather gaunt, mobile face, his white teeth, tanned skin, pale eyes, curly hair, all this and the long raincoat. Cigarette after cigarette. Then, he went out. He didn't want to use the cart or the carriage. The old carriage that trailed the previous century behind it like a long tail. Walter pulled on rubber boots and walked across the frost mirrors, across the frozen bean fields reflected in those mirrors and disappeared along the path that led to the road. From the windowsill where we were watching, we could see the gleam of his raincoat. Where was he going? Would he come back? For four hours, we all thought he would never come back. It occurred to Francisco Dias that a wanderer would always be a wanderer, he wouldn't change. Just as our anxiety was building, from inside the house, we heard the sound of tires. We ran to the windows, went out into the street and saw Walter coming back in a car. A large, immaculate, black Chevrolet, far superior to a taxi. "A car!" they all shouted. Walter Dias, Francisco Dias' youngest son, owned a car.

45.

Yes, it was a black Chevrolet with chrome flashes, gray upholstery, a gleaming dashboard and polished rearview mirror, it was a habitable space, a mobile home to top that day and the excitement of that day. Francisco Dias stood in front of them all, anesthetized, as if he had drunk some potion that made him forget his absent sons. And the journey between West and East took only a day.

The journey has a goal, a vehicle, a driver, passengers, mud, splashes of mud, dirty smudges spoiling the car's brilliant surface. It has a road, it has a route, it has screams of excitement. We, Walter Dias' assorted nephews and nieces, are doing the screaming. During that time, his own daughter does not mind being a niece and she shouts with joy inside the great black barque driven by Uncle Walter who is, in fact, her father. She has no trouble pretending, in exchange for that memorable feeling of joy. "Shall we go?"—he asked, driving out into the muddy road. We were moving. Yes, I am just a niece and I really don't mind. I could be even less, just the first part of the word, or the last, or just a single letter, as long as I was allowed to travel in that car belonging to my father whom I called uncle. My brothers and me. We were all screaming with excitement inside the big car that Walter had brought in the third week of his return to the house in Valmares. A giant automobile, a mastodon with a grille made out of metal like our silver forks, gray suede cushions like gloves. It was something very pure. I remember. If at that time he was traveling with his blanket on the roof rack, as they told me later, I didn't see it. If he put it in the trunk, I never noticed. If an army blanket was traveling with us then, the continent drowned the contents, we ourselves were devoured by that barrel on wheels, by the great covered barque whose concentrated sails lay beneath Walter's feet. No blanket either present or absent mattered. We simply surrendered ourselves, body and soul, to the movement, as if to a swimming stroke that required no effort at all. There we were in the covered space of the big car, piled in together, racing along streets and roads, traveling the N125 at 55 miles an hour, ripping apart, at that furious speed, the paralysis of the fields. Those first days are part of the coming moment, a moment on which everything converges, an approaching season of joy that has not yet arrived, we have not yet taken that bend or even begun to lean into it. The biggest laugh hasn't even been laughed yet, we're bubbling with laughter and we haven't even shouted out with joy yet. We didn't ask why Walter had come now, because we would soon find out. We would know what his objective was.

Yes, the car seemed intended for some purpose. The car was a special place. But despite being such a big car, its volume and capacity were small given the number of passengers being transported. That is, we had never before been so close. That closeness drew us together. That was the objective.

46.

Walter, wearing dark glasses, opened the four doors and ushered us in. He placed two passengers in front and five behind. There was something of the circus about the process of sorting out who would sit where and then getting everyone noisily seated, as if we were entering a golden cage that would carry us back and forth to the house in Valmares. The day laborers stood around, and we clambered in. Francisco Dias got in first, with his youngest grandchild squeezed between his knees on the right-hand seat in front. Then Custódio Dias got in and sat down in the middle of the back seat, followed by Maria Ema and her two other children, their children, the middle ones, and then she, Walter's niece, got in. Maria Ema, with her head resting on the window, was immediately opposite the rearview mirror. Meanwhile, her fifteen-year-old daughter took up her seat on the opposite side on the right, so that she could see who was looking at whom in the mirror, so that she could see Walter Dias. Except the daughter wasn't a daughter, she was a niece. Only then did Walter get in, after the doors had been closed. And so we set off. All united by the same chassis, driven by the same engine, borne along by the same fate. All of us had to get in that car so that Walter and Maria Ema could be but a hand's reach apart. Sitting on the back seat, next to her husband and her children, her knees pressed into the back of the seat in front. Walter asked— "Are you sure you're not uncomfortable?" No, she wasn't uncomfortable. Inside the car, Maria Ema felt very comfortable indeed.

With her sable jacket on her knees, sitting next to her husband and her sons, her hands on the seat in front, she felt comfortable. There she was, with her sable jacket and the voluntary proximity of our bodies and our lives. And so, in February 1963, all together, all crammed into the black barque, its immaculate black chassis spattered with mud, we drove past the flooded fields, the sprouting bean fields, the drowned wheat, the rotting hay, the flourishing weeds, the slimy walls, the crumbling façades. We were traveling together, talking, creating a growing wave of sound, on board a raft, unable to separate, unable to unite. Where had we forged that poisonous bond that bound us? What drew us to the same center, while simultaneously driving us apart? We were traveling, traveling. We set off toward Faro to go shopping, we stopped by the quay to see the seagulls perched on the boats. We took group photographs in which each person was just a small smudge. Then we came back, excited. What was going on inside the car was incomprehensible. Our nearness drove us on, we were a mass of people set adrift, happy, singing, she would talk and he would reply, we arrived back at Valmares, our faces flushed. It was as if inside that great car, Custódio Dias were blind, Francisco Dias numb and Maria Ema's children wild with energy. Everyone wanted to go and see the waves breaking, to see how high the waves were. Walter turned the barque around in the direction of Quarteira. Maria Ema leaned forward and breathed in the sea air, breathed in the perfume of her brother-in-law Walter. We were all deaf and blind. Sometimes they were the only two who did not get out to watch the waves breaking and licking our shoes and socks with tongues of foam. They remained in their seats, sitting very upright, in full view of everyone, not moving, not looking at each other. Still, utterly still, like paralyzed birds. They were waiting for us to return. We arrived shouting and went back home. We were blind, deaf and dumb to that unarticulated reality. We knew nothing and saw nothing.

Francisco Dias went equally mad.

He put on a pair of leather boots with not a hobnail in sight and went down to the kitchen, a place he never went, not even to oversee occasional necessary building work. He burst in and stood between the table, laden with pots, pans and leftovers, and the oven, which was still lit. It was a good place to speak to Alexandrina and tell her that his youngest son had just come back from Canada, or to be precise from a city built by a lake called Ontario. Did she know where that was? It was too complicated to explain. Alexandrina stood astonished amidst the debris of lunch. Her employer said threateningly— "From now on, neither you nor anyone else will call my youngest son a soldier. No one will ever call him soldier Walter again. He has a name like everyone else. His name is Walter Dias, like me, his father," he added, proud of what he was saying. Yes, even Francisco Dias had gone mad.

47.

But it wasn't true. At night, some went madder than others.

Or rather, suddenly, a survival instinct came into play during the cold nights that followed the rain; there was a call to vigilance, an alarm bell in the soul. For the two of them gave off clear, perceptible signals. Maria Ema and Walter Dias prowled the house late at night. Everyone knew about it. Around midnight, she would walk down the corridor carrying an oil lamp in order to fetch a glass of water, and you could hear the warm whisper of her slippers. Downstairs, Walter would go outside, and you would hear the latch on the door fall, then the sharp, metallic click of the Chevrolet door opening. Then he would come back into the house with the cushioned footsteps of his rubber-soled buffalo-skin shoes. Given the two sets of footsteps, they must have seen each other in their dressing gowns. They did see each other. If they didn't, it was as if they did. They were blind. A lightless flash of lightning flickered through the house. Custódio knew. At the time, he and Maria Ema slept in the west room. Maria Ema would get up early, before Custódio, and fill the kettle, then wait by the kettle for it to boil. For no apparent reason, without anyone's going in or coming out, Walter's bedroom door would open and there would be ten, fifteen minutes of absolute silence.

Then we would hear the sound of a clapper hitting only one side of the bell tower, like a lame bell, that is, the sound of Custódio Dias' asymmetric footsteps. Those irregular steps, regular as a pendulum, advanced in the direction of the kitchen. They stopped there. Custódio's footsteps were a deliberate warning. Francisco Dias would appear too, barefoot, in long johns and sheepskin jacket, standing by the far window to draw back the curtains on the weather to come, after the last tremulous star had gone out. The Great Bear and its Keepers. Maria Ema left the kitchen. And Custódio went up the stairs, and again we heard the beat of his blunt foot. Like a bass drum beating out a warning, echoing through the dawn house, unleashing, for their benefit and for his own, everyone's defensive, guardian instinct, for they knew the dangers and risks of that moment. They never made it explicit, but in the darkest dark of their beings, where one feels what cannot be expressed, they knew it was impossible to continue. There'll be a death, they thought, but did not say. Someone will die in this house. Or rather, There's someone here who's superfluous. There was someone, sitting on the bed, who thought what the others were thinking. And the person thinking concluded that the superfluous person was her, the niece, Walter's daughter.

The superfluous person was me.

———

But Walter's daughter put off the obvious consequence of that thought and waited for a bomb to explode, waited for the eighteen-room house to explode in the night. She waited for Francisco Dias suddenly to wake up and send one of his two sons far away and for that son not to be Walter. But nothing like that happened, because we didn't see what everyone saw.

48.

Outside the house, Custódio was again referred to as a cuckold. Custódio knew, but didn't care. We were on our way to mass. The grandfather, the grandchildren, her, the cuckold and me, the whole family or what remained after all the departures, what had been born out of what was left, Francisco Dias' Portuguese family. We were all bundled up.

She was walking in front, wearing her fur jacket, surrounded by her four children, her father-in-law ahead of her in his hobnail boots, Walter and Custódio behind, both wearing buffalo-skin shoes. She had painted her lips cinnamon pink with a touch of orange and a trace of blood, her skin matte, her eyes dark. The human contents of the church were troubled, so were the images. No one dared speak out against something everyone knew to be a crime, although they were unable to say quite where what was forbidden and what was permitted began. The church seethed with disquiet, with suppressed laughter, sideways glances worthy of flies or chameleons. Glances that went from the hands holding the rosaries to the wounded St. Sebastian above the main altar, but they didn't stay there, they immediately swiveled around toward the Dias family, who kept getting up, sitting down, kneeling and crossing themselves like true believers. It was as if the Church of St. Sebastian had been visited by vice incarnate, by corporeal sin, by the spirit of evil disguised as the Dias family, headed by that man, by Walter, who, years before, had been known as soldier Walter. And yet there was distinction in that very inferiority. There was something superior about the situation, which rebuffed those glances, which repudiated and kept at a distance the buzz of rumor. The Dias family were the interpreters of a battle in progress, of a fight to the finish, both in defense of itself and in forgiveness of itself, carried to the furthest extreme. A proof that the world had been conceived in sin. *"Ora pro nobis"*—I said, before they did. And then we got up, turned and knelt for the last time, all together like a single being, like a sick animal that does not realize its wounds are visible to everyone. More than that, we walked slowly back to the car, got in, displayed the four open doors of the Chevrolet and took our places in our by now customary circus fashion. And we left. Everyone knew that an original sin hung over the family, that we were overshadowed, branded by a giant octopus that had escaped the pack.

49.

And after mass came Sunday afternoon, and the radio was blasting out music. Walter called out—"Dance music!" The radio is playing dance music. I can hear the dance music of that Sunday afternoon in March 1963. Custódio came downstairs with his blunt foot and found Walter surrounded by his three small sons. Francisco Dias went over to the radio and looked at the box to see if the music was real. Dance music. Custódio Dias called upstairs—"Maria Ema, they're playing dance music—a bolero." Maria Ema came downstairs, sat in a chair and stared at the radio. Her foot tapped against the leg of the chair. Dance music! But no one could dance. Walter moved a couple of chairs back and pretended to be dancing with a partner. Custódio said to Walter—"Why don't you dance with her?" Walter took Maria Ema's arm, she cupped her left hand and placed it on his shoulder and gave him her right hand. Custódio pushed the sofas and other chairs back against the wall to make a larger space. They took up the middle of that space, and what remained was taken up by Custódio and Maria Ema's three children, who crawled on all fours on the floor, swaying their bodies like cats in heat. The children arranged themselves face-to-face and circled around, like quadrupeds dancing. Maria Ema and Walter, their arms about each other, crossed the room from side to side, avoiding the children. Custódio finally lost patience with the children and removed them from the center of the space, shoving them up against the chairs, then roughly ordered them to sit down and keep still. He had only just managed to corral his children when the radio announced the dance music program was about to end. Custódio and Maria Ema's children started hitting each other, and Custódio cuffed each of them around the head, and Maria Ema, newly emerged from that position of constrained light-ness close to Walter, also turned on the children, slapping them. One of the children began to cry softly, then more loudly, then to bawl, and the other two joined in so that no one heard the end of the program—*Ladies and gentlemen, on another peaceful Sunday afternoon, you have just been listening to our regular program of dance music. Join us again next Sunday . . .*

50.

It happened the following day.

In the middle of the single, glorious day that constituted Walter's visit, woven, of course, out of various nights and days. The dance music had suggested another direction for our trips in the Chevrolet. What if we headed west this time? Yes, why not?

So we headed west. Again we traveled, leaning to one side on the curves and righting ourselves as we bounded along the straightaways. The great car, en route to the West, carried us past fields, hills, mountains, sober scrubland, gnarled olive trees, stunted fig trees, and everything moved to one side, opening up as we passed, as the black car passed, bearing us off toward the great, historic promontory of Sagres, of which all any of us had ever seen was the light from the lighthouse. We set off as if on a picnic, with a basket of fruit and a camera slung over the shoulder, and suddenly, the car stopped, we got out, the sky grew vast, we walked across a field of stones and stood before the abyss.

Francisco Dias could not believe that a point of land, which was, after all, attached to the same piece of land where he had his house and his farm, could contain such an abyss. The wind was blowing. The sea was beating far below and the spume rose up. We went to see the magnifying lens of the lighthouse. The great glass lens. It was like some supreme object. We were all lost for words. We were all utterly astonished. The lens was an arrow pointing into the abyss. The lens in the shape of a moon split in two was like another heavenly body. It blazed with light, it burned with its cold brilliance. The lighthouse keeper was talking. He was talking about the end of the Continent and the discovery of the New World, everything Walter had already told us and which was no longer of any interest to us. We did not want to know that long ago, lost in the long, long ago, you could have stepped across the distance separating Sagres and Long Island. That the surface of the Earth was one, floating on one side of the globe, but we weren't interested in that geographical lecture. We were only interested in the abyss. The glass half-moon was merely a forefinger pointing to the abyss. We left and the wind seemed to want to carry us off toward nameless places. A place where the sea was no longer called the Atlantic and was just an infinite mass of water, adrift, where the land ceased to be a province or a continent, a road or a city and was simply land. The elements around us were all howling for a return to antiquity, roaring, pushing us, catching at our clothes and pointing to the abyss. All we had to do was make our way back into the black car, like someone returning to the dark uterus, walking quickly back, fleeing from that place that was drawing us down into the depths of the sea, that wedge-shaped piece of land against which the noisy waves were beating. We fled. And then the passenger in the sable jacket, instead of running like us toward the car, ran in the opposite direction, toward the promontory, over which the wind passed without a murmur, strong, indomitable, invisible, like a temptation. We saw her from the car. We saw Maria Ema take off her high heels, tear off her jacket and approach the edge. Custódio managed to limp a few steps in her direction, the wind snatching at his hair, but the first person to reach the final rib of the promontory was Walter Dias. It was Walter who brought her back, brushed down her jacket, put her in the car, in the front seat, who quieted her sobs and drew her back from the abyss. From that abyss. We returned now, with everyone in different places. In front of us all, he stroked her hair, held her hand when the road was straight, placed her hand beneath his to change gear. He caressed her in front of all of us, unashamedly, boldly, as if there were no witnesses, as if the backs of their two seats formed a screen hiding them from the world. The world that was sitting behind them. The dumbstruck world. Her small sons were dumbstruck, not knowing where to look. There were six of us in the back. All of us dumbstruck. We were all piled in together, on top of each other, we were a clump of unhappy cattle going back to the Valmares house in a hearse.

We could never get back in that car again.

51.

He parked the car beside the wagon. There was hatred in Walter's pale eyes, as if over some unjustifiable death.

I can see those same eyes at dawn the following morning. I can hear him getting up, opening the front door, lighting the oil lamp, dragging furniture around, clumsily opening drawers, walking about outside in the dark. I can see him beneath the colors of that dying night, which, at this moment, is tonight, is any night, the leaves fallen from the almond trees form a fine, soft carpet along the paths surrounding the house. This house. The gleam of his raincoat betrays his presence along the muddy paths. Walter is dressed and ready. He is dragging objects out of the junk room. He is pulling out papers, clothes, broken boxes, broken basins, hoe handles, and throwing them on the ground. He drags the buggy roughly, noisily out of the junk room and chops it into pieces with an ax. As dawn comes, you can hear the ax cutting into the buggy, you can hear him dragging bits of it away, hear him pushing the chassis down the slope, hear the hood dangling from it fall with a crash. Wheels, shafts, planks, yoke—all in a heap. The windows of the Valmares house are open to the dawn chill. Alexandrina and Blé even approach with a lantern, even exchange a few words, but then draw back, move away, and, like us, lean against the walls and watch Walter's struggle. We know what is going to happen. Suddenly, in the midst of the unseasonable cold of that March dawn, flames rise, lighting up the front of the house and the courtyard. Walter is leaving, destroying his tracks, he will never return to this house.

And meanwhile I can still see him in the lights and shadows cast by the fire, in the cold, in the mirror of melting frost. The smooth water running over the mud. The crystals of cold, like a window, shattering. I can still hear him leaving. He will set off before daybreak and he won't come back. Nothing of Walter Dias will come back to this house apart from rumors about the legend of his arrival and his departure, all so recent and yet told as vaguely as if the stories dated from the Middle Ages. Of himself there will only be news from a distance, the news of his different drawings, depending on the places he is traveling through, and finally his blanket will return to confirm the silence. The wall of the West had descended over the Atlantic, opposite which, amidst stony hills, strips of sand and rubble, we had our home. We still do. What does that mean, "our home"?

But I went down and stood in his way. I placed my body in front of the wheels and he got out of the car.

He clasped me to him, to the raincoat scorched by his struggle and by the fire, and I gathered up the warmth of his neck and of his hair falling over his collar, his breath, his perfume. I gathered them all up and poured them into a deep cup. The final images of Walter at Valmares rise up from the damp morning, like steam from ice, struggling to the surface of the water. A fire made during the night, a fire still burning as morning broke. I imagine him like a flame. A timid but persistent flame in the dawn sunlight. The windows are open. Everyone, including Maria Ema, is looking out of the windows, but no one dares utter a single word, as if the abyss had disguised itself by putting on different foam and different rocks in a different place. Then came the silence.

52.

How could Walter have said, only days before, on that rainy night, that he had given me nothing? I inherited the murmurous life of what happened before the silence. I became heir to the image of their love affair and of the intense passion that was a consequence of their incompatibility. That image crosses the silence of many years, ten, twenty, thirty years, then the car, which still moves over that thin film, arrives and stops, wrapped in silence. A comfortable ghost. Maria Ema and Walter are inside the car, even though I know they never traveled alone in it. The Kodak snaps prove it. We took photos, and the pictures remain, like curved roof tiles. Maria Ema and Walter never together, always apart. Walter and I apart too. He and I always far from each other, just like her. Perhaps I was her or he was I, I don't know, no one will ever know, unless on some distant day, our secret is transformed and the mystery of love, hidden and buried beneath the earth, flowers in some other place.

Because she should have got rid of me in order to be herself during the woman's life she deserved to have, but she didn't. She didn't know how to, she had neither the ways nor the means. She didn't know what steps she could take to get rid of the child curled inside her. That is why she had allowed things to go on longer than she wanted, and I took on that dead part of her. There we were, she and I, far from him. I was always far from him. Separated by various heads, we did not look like father and daughter as we had in that first photograph, we no longer had the same halo of tightly curled hair. My face had gone off in another direction. In the rigorous winter of 1963, I tamed my hair with oil and a hot hair dryer, uncurling it, wanting to be different, which is why I no longer looked like him. But when I stood nearer to him, we would re-create that image of resemblance. Besides, we had tested it out on that rainy night, standing in front of the long, seaweed-thin mirror. Our disheveled hair was lit by the light of the oil lamp and he said to me—"God, we're so alike!"

If it hadn't been for me, Maria Ema would be with Walter, and Custódio Dias would have had children by another woman, and my brothers would be the sons of Maria Ema Baptista and Walter Glória Dias. Perhaps only they would have existed, not me. I was the child of a chance moment, an impulse, a wrong turning, of raw youth and physical exuberance. No, I would not exist, only my three brothers, their children, born of their good sense and their love, and there would have been more space in the car because my place would be unoccupied, because I would not exist. So I was responsible for that black barque arriving at our door only to sink without trace. I was guilty, I was responsible for a responsibility that went far deeper than guilt, because it was born out of a state created before I even existed, an inherited condition that had made me in the image of guilt itself. Pools, clouds, beaches, road junctions, all the places we had passed were places where I should have apologized for existing, cardinal points that indicated ways of succumbing, by leaving or disappearing into the endless distance. A repellent guilt, a guilt greater than us, as sordid as a slow suicide, and yet I allowed myself to continue to exist. Fifteen years. In order for me to exist, those years made a pact of silence with whatever powers might be.

That is why, when we were in the car, I never spoke, I only yelled, not once did I address him directly, I had never spoken directly to anyone, not even to my brothers. We hit and punched each other, and they bandied insults, but I never called out to them, just as if I weren't there. Even during the delicious hours spent traveling in the car, I had made a supreme effort to be neither present nor absent, so that they would not feel the weight of my existence, so that my guilt would not increase. Inside the car, I always kept silent, like someone keeping firm hold of a dragon, knowing that, should it get free, we would all be destroyed. Now the last morning was beginning, and the silence was pierced by a noise, the noise of wheels, and that noise was like a closed ring made up of cold and silence.

53.

Besides, the word was hers, Maria Ema's. She had requested my silence, before Walter had even arrived.

After getting up from the bed, after that scene in which she had torn her silk dress, when she was beginning to surrender to the joy of waiting for Walter like someone surrendering to the euphoria of an innocuous drug, bound once more to life with all the force of her thirty-odd years, Maria Ema had come looking for me, with the photo of Walter and myself in her hand. I knew she might begin with that photo she kept hidden in unexpected places, but Maria Ema was showing it to me before Walter arrived because she wanted to ask me a favor, in the name of my three brothers and of Custódio Dias. The favor was as follows. She wanted me to be sure always to call Walter Dias "Uncle." She asked me, please, for the love of God, never to get it wrong. What would it cost me to replace the two syllables of "father" with those of "uncle"? she asked. I must, please, consider her request, I must collaborate and never make a slip. "No mistakes, please!"—she said, her eyes shining urgently. Maria Ema wanted me to be kind and helpful and to participate in the welcome party, but my main contribution would be my discretion and my silence and, above all, my use of the word "uncle." She was counting on me. And we understood each other. We hardly ever spoke and yet we were so close that, suddenly, standing by the window, we looked at each other and we were the same age. It wasn't very cold, even though we were still only in the first few days of January 1963. Yes, from that day forth, we sealed our pact of silence and collaboration, and now, in front of the black car, knowing he was leaving, I was collaborating with his departure. Maria Ema had asked for discretion and silence, hadn't she? Well, here was the silence. It arrived at the end of winter with the departure of Walter Dias.

Yes, the hour of silence had arrived, the century of silence, he was starting it with the noise of the bonfire in the empty field next to the scrawny bean field, on the sandy, barren slopes where we had our yard. Where we still have our yard. The silence pointed a finger at what was going to happen, it pointed to the future of the land. The silence was pointing with its finger at what was about to happen, at the direction the future of the land would take. The silence was saying that heaven would be like that. A great space filled by nothing, where no one would remember anything, where there would be no one to remember anything. In heaven nothing would exist. No desire, no pain, no memory of any affection. That is what heaven would be like. The streams would be frozen, the clouds absent, everything would come to resemble nothing. Heaven would be nothing. How good, that heaven should be an annihilated space where man's toil was unnecessary, that love should exist in its stillest, purest state. That would be heaven. It was not like that here on earth, not yet. We still moved around like animals, we still built roads, everything was still in motion, even if there were no more purpose to our existence than to die after having existed and to have existed further and further back in time up to the point when we did not exist at all. Yes, that is what heaven would be like. On that morning, Francisco Dias' house was beginning to resemble heaven, Walter Dias' daughter would think later on and write the thought down in her school notebooks, protected as she was by the revolver, left by her father, not left behind, but left. Voluntarily given. I remember that silence, that progress in the direction of the reality of the world and the density of matter. I remember trying to push against the silence. And it was in the swift motion we had experienced inside the car that I looked for the sounds that used to exist and that drove me on. They were born out of a desire to re-create the soft pad of Walter's footsteps. He was coming in from the inhospitable courtyard. We were still in February, in the grip of the surprise, of those drives along the N125, at the very peak of all the joy, the waves, the speed and the group intoxication that touched even Francisco Dias.

54.

Yes, the silence had been by agreement with Maria Ema. But at the height of all the joy, her daughter had also felt the desire to go beyond the narrow limits in which she moved and to surrender to the euphoria of breaking her promise.

Her transgression consisted in waiting for him each night when he parked the Chevrolet under the porch in the courtyard and came into the house through the side door. The route to the living room meant that Walter had to walk along the corridor of transom windows. She would slowly open the door of her room at the top of the stairs, just a crack, and watch him walk swiftly past, helped by those buffalo-skin shoes that seemed to have no weight and no fixed form and that carried him rapidly out of sight. She would watch him on his way to the living room and to his own bedroom, a kind of bulky shadow to be gathered in, and the next day, the joy would start all over again, for that was the only moment when he, unwittingly, shared something private and unique with her. He shared with her the walk he took along the corridor, without turning around. She started to place herself just inside the half-open door to savor the moment all the more. She didn't need him to say anything, or see her or even turn around— Don't stop, don't look, don't see me . . .

And one night, he did turn around and saw her standing at the door–Don't look at me, don't see me, don't come upstairs . . . And the next night, he turned and saw her in the same place–Don't stop, walk on, don't see me or call to me . . . And he had stood there for a moment. From then on, Walter began to walk along the corridor with even lighter steps, deadening the sound of his rubber soles, and from her position at the top of the stairs, she thought, He doesn't need to see me or to stop or to come upstairs . . . And yet she stood at the half-open door, waiting. She would open the door before Walter began his walk, placing herself on the threshold, by the light, in order to be present at that moment. No, don't ever come upstairs. But if you did want to come up, if you did come up . . . , she thought, never moving from the corner lit by the oil lamp.

And that rainy night, when the falling water offered a rare protecting veil, and when everyone else was asleep in their rooms, she thought it would be a good night for him to visit her, and so she did not stand at the door, but stayed inside the room, waiting. She had the idea it was an impudent thing to do, a guilty desire, almost a sin, and yet she waited for Walter, silent as a shadow, to come and see her. And so it happened. He had come up the stairs and come into the room without knocking, in his stocking feet, with his shoes in one hand, and he had reached for the oil lamp. "Please, don't call out! Don't move!"–he had said. She didn't need to say a word and, even if she had needed to, she couldn't have. He had stayed with her for two and a half hours, possibly three. Custódio had appeared, marking the darkness with his unmistakable footsteps and his flashlight, but the niece could rest easy. No one would ever know that Walter Dias had visited his daughter. The sound of his footsteps on the bedroom floor formed a circle sealed with a diamond padlock inside her silence. So she thought.

55.

That is why, on that morning, while Walter was loading up the black Chevrolet with the two marked suitcases and the bags bearing the name of the airline with which he had traveled, she ran over to the car. She stood in front of the wheels, in the middle of the courtyard, stopping him from leaving. And Francisco Dias, who was at one of the windows, said—"Get her away from there!" But no one did. On the contrary. I can remember it as if it were happening now. They were all standing at the windows, leaning on the windowsills, and among them was Maria Ema. In front of the house, the fire gives off a smell of wood, charcoal and calamity, of burned objects consumed in the air. The daughter goes down and stands in front of the car. And he tries to shift her, he even says he wants to take her with him. He says that in Canada the buildings are enormous and the roads cross snowfields that stretch farther than the eye can see. That life is generous, free, different. He has time to say all this as they stand in front of the Chevrolet. He tells her to get in, he tells her that Toronto is an unimaginably flat city. Right there, he spreads out before her a distant civilization, a place of frugality, fortune, wealth, profit and experience, where she can have a brilliant future and an English-speaking boyfriend. Far away. In the middle of the courtyard, he brandishes before her the solemnly glittering words "far away," as if he had not repeated them countless times on the night he had visited her. Yes, she knows. He grips her wrists, tries to force her into the car—"Get in quickly, go on!" As if they were alone, as if it were happening during that rainy night, except that he doesn't take off his shoes, he doesn't walk around silently, he's not afraid of anyone's footsteps on that morning in Valmares. On the contrary, Walter says out loud—"Get in, please, for God's sake, get in. Don't stay here any longer!"

But she is fifteen and already an old woman. She has already imagined a hundred thousand suns rising and the same number setting, and that is why she knows that the plot is written, and like a very old woman with a paralyzed soul, she knows she must stay where she is, she knows it is best not to get in the car. According to the ancient girl's identity card, she is fifteen, but it's not true. The ancient girl is a very old woman. She has a century inside her head, possibly more, she has the beginning of *The Iliad* behind her eyelids, she has an infinite number of Achaean and Trojan dead on her tongue, she has the ending of that book in her head, and she knows that, for millions of years now, everything has been mingled together on a beach beneath nine layers of sand. So she knows it is not worth taking even one step in order to change, the play will be the same. To run on ahead would merely be to run straight into what she had left behind. She still thinks, though, that the black barque of the Chevrolet cannot proceed without her, that Walter will not pass. That he will be unable to leave, with his headlights off, down the short track that leads to the road. That is what the ancient girl still thinks. Until she moves away from in front of the car, and he leaps in and drives off without a backward glance. That afternoon, she will plunge into the ancient words and confirm that everything is the same. That everything comes from an ancient wound and that everything goes back to that. A crack. At the table in her room, emerging from that crack thanks to the power of words, she reads out loud to herself—"*the saffron veil of Aurora spread over the earth, and they advanced on the city...*" For he really did want to take her away from there. Walter will always think that by changing places, you change yourself. On that morning, the point of departure was this place where we are now. I inherited Walter's departure in 1963. I inherited it intact and indivisible. That is why, tonight, Walter Dias does not have to come upstairs feeling guilty and apologetic, nor should he have written the dry words he wrote in that forward-sloping hand of his—*I leave to my niece, as sole inheritance, this soldier's blanket.*

56.

The days that followed were a time of circumspection, espionage and evaluation of the silence. I see those weeks like a rehearsal during which the formless body of the unspoken first began to emerge. Besides, it wasn't necessary to speak. Walter Dias had left because he couldn't get what he wanted, though he had never said what that was, and yet now what he had wanted was as clear to everyone as a public announcement.

Maria Ema was there before us, like a naked figure, clothed in transparency, as if she were an object bound for an exhibition. As defenseless as an object placed in the middle of the living room for all to see. Her nakedness was so real, so genuine, it made one feel like grabbing the tablecloth and covering not only her body but her very being, to release her from our gaze, to steal her from under our own eyes.

Francisco Dias looked at her, disoriented, as if only in some posthumous way had he realized what was going on inside his own house. Custódio dealt with Maria Ema's nakedness like someone fussing over a piece of blown glass in danger of melting or evaporating. For him she was as fragile as glass. Alexandrina and Blé could not even look at her, they came and went with eyes lowered, but they noticed how rarely she changed her clothes, how little she ate, how little time she spent with her children. And yet, at first, as regards her work around the house, Maria Ema behaved quite normally. She bent over the fire, sat up again, read magazines, the *Selecções Femininas* she got through the mail, the romantic novels she subscribed to. But apart from those, the mailman, who arrived by bicycle, brought nothing else. He brought no letters for Custódio Dias, nor the drawings that used to accompany them. After a few weeks, she went and sat by the side of the road, unashamedly waiting for the bicycle to pass. The mailman would arrive, leave the odd dull bit of mail and then disappear round the bend behind the trees, which were magnificent at that time of year. Then Maria Ema got hay fever and retired to her bed. We could see what would happen. None of us knew when Maria Ema Baptista was likely to get up again. I can see her now. I remember her on this night when Walter came in through the door again, as he did on that other rainy night. I see her submerged in blankets.

No, I can't even see her.

In bed, with the bedcovers up to her neck, Maria Ema wears fewer and fewer clothes, she is naked to the waist, to the crotch, to another even more shameful part of the soul than that, a part more intimately bound up with her being, more intimate and internal even than her own uterus. Maria Ema's soul is bare. The longer she lies there, thinking herself hidden in the darkness of her room, huddled in blankets too heavy for the spring outside exploding in light and pollen, with the sainfoin drying, the broad beans turning black, hanging from their hollow stalks, the more visible she is. After a few weeks, someone opens the window in her room. They are sisters and cousins, older women, who approach authoritatively and take turns attending her. Some live in Faro, others in Lisbon, they left the area some years ago and return at Custódio's request, armed with energy to save her. Their bouffant hairdos, four tall towers crisp with lacquer, gather determinedly around Maria Ema. The heels of their shoes echo around the house like those of nurses in the empty wing of a hospital. They rummage through drawers, open windows, try to entice her out of bed, to make her get up, unable to understand how Walter's visit could have laid her so low. In the opinion of her sisters Dulce and Quitéria, she is lovesick for a good-for-nothing, a dishonored man, and it's entirely her own fault if she hasn't the courage to see this. In the opinion of her cousins, both called Zulmira, the fault is his.

He is full of negative energy, which he knows how to use to dire effect. Walter is one of those people who feed off the lives of others. They suck out the soul and energy of the weakest, the way vampires drink the blood of their defenseless victims. The Zulmiras imagine Walter, wherever he is, making his way in the world at the expense of those he came here to suck dry. According to the cousins' authorized version, Walter's vampire self is, at that very moment, feeding off the lives of Maria Ema, Custódio Dias, old Francisco Dias, and even the children to whom he has brought nothing but disquiet and ruin. Her sisters and her cousins remove the blankets, heave her desperately out of bed, try to make her breathe some fresh air—"Why don't you fight back?"

But Maria Ema refused to get up and she didn't want them to open the windows. When she did move, she did so unsteadily, she didn't want to eat, she didn't want to go for a walk. She would have liked to behave differently, but she couldn't. Custódio Dias was the one who took the children to school, using the cart. He would leave them at the train station and come back, indifferent to those who laughed at him and called him cuckold. The cuckold would come home and sit at Maria Ema's bedside. I see that image again, that mystery, that tender misunderstanding, that brute sentiment, that brow adorned by an inappropriate crown. And I remember the night when she seemed to want to give up, as if she were a princess in a fairy tale, before the words "neurasthenia" and "depression" existed, only "sadness" or, at most, "prostration" or "melancholy." I remember the night when they found her coming out of the stables with a piece of rope in her hand, staring fascinated at the trunk of the loquat tree. Francisco Dias was shouting–"Go on, let her kill herself!" But Custódio started phoning various doctors' offices until he found the home number of a doctor known as Dr. Dalila.

57.
Dr. Dalila came on that May night.

He arrived around midnight.

I remember the moonlit night when Custódio phoned the man with his black bag. Walter's daughter remembers everything or almost everything, because she was standing at the door of the room. The doctor sat down on a chair without saying a word, and he looked at the person before him, a young woman lying in bed with the blankets pulled up to her chin, refusing to get up. He began questioning the patient, but she didn't reply, she didn't even turn to look at him, and when he asked the same questions of Custódio, Custódio simply covered his eyes with his hand and said nothing. Dr. Dalila started to laugh, then he stopped and said that only when things are at their worst can they begin to mend. That the cure lay in ourselves, but that some people were able to use that ability to cure themselves and others weren't. And the doctor gave a satisfied laugh. He deserved his reputation as incompetent, ill-informed, ineffectual and incapable of making a diagnosis; when he left, he nearly forgot his bag. I remember that he left without drama, remorse or prescription. Walter's daughter was at the door and she saw Dr. Dalila leave. But he said to Custódio Dias—"You can call me at any time of night. I'm always awake."

And the following night, Dalila came back without anyone's having called him. And he came the following night and the night after that. The moon changed from full to waning, from waning to new and back to its first quarter, and every night, before midnight, Dr. Dalila would come. Francisco Dias would shout—"Let her die!" But Custódio carefully counted the steps Maria Ema had taken, the interest she had shown in this or that subject, the amount of food she had eaten. He spoke in whispers, because he did not want anyone else to know, he did not want it talked about in Valmares. And Dr. Dalila would stare around vaguely at the objects in the room and say—"Fine, fine, keep at it"—and then he would leave. It didn't seem to make much difference if he came or not, and yet, Maria Ema's salvation was on its way to find her in the person of Dr. Dalila. It took an oddly comical form, embedded in the silence following Walter's departure, but that didn't matter. Salvation was on its way.

58.

Dr. Dalila lived in a house surrounded by fig trees. It was odd that a doctor, who was far from being an old man, should live hidden away in a such a house and should only be available to call on patients at night. His house was near the cliffs and the main door was an iron grille which had no latch. Maria Ema's daughter was coming back from the beach as night was falling, her books tied together with a leather strap and slung over her shoulder. She stopped outside Dr. Dalila's house and stood looking at the gray courtyard deep in dead leaves, the house closed up in the dark of dusk, with no car at the door. But then a car pulled up behind Maria Ema's daughter; it was Dr. Dalila.

She particularly remembered that night. It was still early, not yet time for the doctor to visit his patient in Valmares. So he and his patient's daughter had time to talk. By the sea. The two of them set off in Dr. Dalila's blue car.

She remembers the sea that night, a smooth sea, cut in two by a ribbon of brilliant, silver moonlight, and Dr. Dalila sitting at a table outside a shack, supposedly a bar, the walls lined with sleepy flies and decorated with dried octopus. She remembers the obscure bar and Dr. Dalila explaining his name. He had a proper name, a different name and was a specialist in maxillo-facial surgery. But he preferred to have a pseudonym and to live off small jobs, quick house calls, and to relate to human beings as whole people, not just jaws and faces. He preferred to laugh, to treat life as a game. He was fun. Out of the bar, from amidst the stationary flies, came glasses of whisky poured from his own personal bottle, which was kept there and bore a label with his name on it, not his real name, but that of Dr. Dalila. And the same happened the next day and the next. Maria Ema could never have imagined that her salvation lay in that seaside meeting between Walter's daughter and a bottle that Dr. Dalila was emptying as if sipping from a still. She could never even have imagined that meeting. Walter's daughter remembers the comical route taken by that meeting and that salvation.

Two weeks later, the ribbon of the sea was not quite so bright, it was a new moon again. Nevertheless, the fig trees pointed the way to Dr. Dalila's house, flanking the sandy track that led to the iron grille, and when the car stopped, and a door with a wooden bar opened for the first time to Walter Dias' daughter, she was confronted by a ramshackle house that did not seem like a doctor's house at all. If it weren't for a desk and a pharmocopoeia, the house could have been home to an unemployed blacksmith or a truck driver. In the midst of the disorder were a couple of sofas covered with bedspreads, excellent for sleeping on he said. He drew Walter's daughter to him and soothed her in a calm, slow, rather sweet voice, slightly slurred by whisky. He asked her, please, not to move away, he couldn't do anything to her, he was as harmless as a woman. Luckily for her, he had become a woman. And he laughed at himself and at her, a vague, consoling laugh. His body was, in fact, that of a bony woman without breasts or rounded buttocks, but otherwise no different, apart from the hair and the smell. Walter's daughter was curious about that figure on the sofa, that naked *majo*, that eunuch, sitting, with a glass in his hand, looking at her, wanting her, undressing her. She remembers his longing, his painful, avid gaze, remembers Dr. Dalila's soft hands, his wet mouth, his flushed forehead. She remembers the hours that passed during the month of June, before his nightly visit to Valmares at the wheel of his blue car. But only after some weeks did Maria Ema receive her strange cure. We all needed one. Finally, a touch of comedy came to our aid.

59.

Walter's daughter began arriving home, her clothes rumpled and her books torn, alongside Dr. Dalila, and while Custódio discussed the progress his wife was making, Maria Ema would sit up in bed and look from her daughter to the doctor and back again. Her eyes went from one to the other, filled with such horror, with such evident affliction it was almost grotesque. And the cure for Maria Ema's lovesickness—whose form and outcome descended from a type long out of fashion and rarely described or depicted except, perhaps, in some ancient Mexican film—came about on the night or, rather, at the bizarre midnight hour when she herself stood waiting for the doctor at the door of the house.

Custódio was at the door to the courtyard. "Good evening, Doctor"–he said. To be honest, on that occasion, he had no idea how many steps his wife had taken around the house, nor how many spoonfuls of rice she had eaten, nor what topics of conversation she had shown some interest in. But there was no need to hear Custódio Dias' report, because Maria Ema was there at the door, dressed and with her shoes on, having recovered her circumspection, and despite the red-hot bricks of the house in Valmares in that scalding late July, she was leaning against one of the walls, waiting, her hands clenched and her mouth tight shut. An unexpected energy filled Maria Ema's neurasthenic pulses. The patient walked straight over to Dr. Dalila's car, dragged her daughter out and hit her hard, knocking her to the ground.

For the first time in her life, she hit her.

She was the image of Walter Dias, she screamed, and, like him, she was corrupt and depraved, false and deceitful, treacherous and immoral. Now she understood why she had so loved to ride in the Devil's Chariot when she was a little girl. Custódio grasped her furiously by the wrists, and her sons approached, astonished at this uproar, which they would never have thought possible in that house inhabited by their mother's silence. Francisco Dias was saying—"Go on, let them kill each other!" But none of that mattered—Maria Ema was safe. In that strange way, she was saving herself from her love for Walter Dias.

She was saved because, from that day on, she assumed the role of guard, of gargoyle, spy, protector, overseer, guardian of customs, and guardian of her daughter's sensuality, lips, breasts and legs, of her daughter's whole body. She watched her footsteps, where she went, watched for any rapid movements she might make, watched to see if she sprayed herself with perfume, watched her straight, tamed, waist-length hair, she was the guardian of her salvation for some future marriage and the guardian of herself in the guise of another body. So Dr. Dalila would never again visit the house in Valmares, but then he didn't need to. Now Maria Ema's medicine consisted in the absence of her daughter, who, during the whole month of August, regularly set off in the direction of the beach, for a ramshackle house surrounded by fig trees. I evoke that time of silence among the fig trees, so that, tonight, Walter will know.

60.

Walter Dias' daughter would lie down on the sofa while Dr. Dalila slept soundly, and she would lean against him and read, dab at the corners of his mouth and sometimes she would doze off too, but around eight o'clock they would both wake up. He would take a bath and so would she, and then they would lie with their arms around each other—"You see? I really am as harmless as a woman." The month of August sped past. Dalila went away for a few weeks and when he came back, he was slightly fatter and more agile; he still drank whisky as voraciously and devotedly as before, but he seemed to have done without it while he was away, or to have been drinking a different kind of whisky. One afternoon, after a nap, around the end of September, Dr. Dalila ceased being as harmless as a woman. Amidst the rubbish, the screwed-up bits of paper and the open bag of medical equipment, he was transformed back into a man and he possessed Walter's daughter. And that is all there is to say about it.

Except that Maria Ema was waiting for her at the door in Valmares, waiting in order to protect her. And her daughter did as she was bidden—she gave her mother plenty of reasons to protect her. Her worldly cynicism was now as palpable as a bag of fruit to be weighed on Francisco Dias' scales, or as a road being bulldozed through the sand. On the night of Dalila's first offensive, her daughter came back at dawn, exuberant, with her shoes in her hand and her clothes covered in dark stains–"Where have you been? What have you been doing?" After a few days, Maria Ema summoned Walter's daughter and told her loudly what kind of man Dr. Dalila was—a drunk and a lecher. Maria Ema now prayed for protection for her daughter, but she was so far beyond her reach, so quick, so evasive, that she could only appeal to someone beyond the windows and rooftops, someone who moved more quickly than Dr. Dalila's car. That was how Maria Ema began, out loud, to ask God for his protection. The placid autumn of 1963.

I remember her pleas, remember how she stood at the windows of the house in Valmares and called on God–Lord God, please don't let Dr. Dalila touch my daughter, make my daughter feel only disgust for Dr. Dalila, don't let him take her out in his car, don't let him be intimate with her, don't let him touch her arms, her skin, don't let him touch her hair. Dear God, protect her from him, from his shadow, from his breath. She prayed, but when five o'clock in the afternoon struck, she knew that God could not help her. Her daughter would leave the house by the back door and walk toward the sea, along the road lined with agaves, but she never got as far as the beach. She would turn to the right and follow the road lined with fig trees, open the iron grille with no latch and go in. God was not moved by Maria Ema's pleas. Thus began not only the decade of silence and its accompanying burlesque, but also its synthesis, the decade of irony.

Don't let her fall into temptation, into curiosity, into dissolution, into the indifference of the body, the delicious passivity of the body, the reveling in the dust of mortal sin, the plunge into the dark, the open hand of lust. That is how Maria Ema learned to pray, from a little book, in the winter of 1964.

Or more specifically—"Free her from him, from the drunkard inside him, from the drunken children who might exist in his body and be passed into my daughter's body"—she would say, looking out of the window, moved by a barbarous realism, a vulgar admonition which, meanwhile, was saving her. So Dr. Dalila served a useful purpose.

61.

I invoke the decade of irony, the decade of silence pierced by the oblique laughter of cynicism, and Maria Ema at the window of the house in Valmares, watching in case her daughter went out, and sometimes she did and sometimes she didn't, according to her mood. Going out, years later, in the direction of the fig trees, but not now to the house of fig trees, but to other houses and other places. Boardinghouses, beaches, boats. Because, after a few years, Dalila too disappeared. Nothing grave or painful happened, he simply disappeared.

I remember his disappearance, one Carnival Tuesday. It was as if Dr. Dalila were dressed for Carnival, as if nothing in his life were serious, and the flesh were merely his emblematic element. Dalila had not seen what was actually before him for some time now. Regardless of what he picked up, it was always a glass. He suffered from the moment he woke. He would get up, identify the objects containing the relevant liquid and sit down in front of a glass, which grew steadily redder. He would pick up the bottle, pour himself a glass, raise it in the air and say—"To my last drink!" As if that really were the last one. But he was toasting a last drink that would never exist in his day or in his life. His problem lay in the idea he had of what constituted the last drink. Walter's daughter would watch with fascination that glass which was supposed to be his last. Why shouldn't it be his last? She would grab it from him and hold it up saying—"This is your last drink, Dalila!" He would take the glass from her and reply—"Yes, the last one before the last." Because he already had the last one in his hand. Between a last drink and another last drink lay a man's defeat. Walter's daughter would look at the two glasses and wish that the last one could go back one glass, because it was only a difference of one, the difference of willpower kicking in before and not after the last in the series. It was as if the series had broken down and the last one kept being reproduced ad infinitum. The window of that cave looked out on to the waves, and the daughter could see in them an infinite series of gestures like Dalila's. Each wave that rolled into the beach was the last of an infinite series of last waves that had followed, one after the other, ever since the dawn of time. Between the last and the last was the time when we had emerged, between two waves, two lasts. Two last drinks. A breakdown. She went back inside and held out the latest last glass to the doctor, and another last and another. The last would only come with Dalila's death. She was grateful to him and to Walter, who had placed in her path, like a magnificent legacy, the ability to understand the power of the penultimate. There was no need to say thank you, but she did, breaking the silence, piercing the silence with a glass arrow.

Dalila used to ask—"Don't you mind the fact that I'm harmless as a woman?" And Walter's daughter would say no. And he would think she was lying and would weep softly over his last half-full glass—always half-full—for the lie he thought she was telling him. There among the fig trees, on the flat clifftop, facing the sea, the wild land, the ambiguous beach, the dying fishing industry. "I'll just have one last drink, then I'll go back on the wagon...I'll start all over again, I'll be a new man, I'll exercise and go running, and I won't be a harmless old woman anymore. I'll marry you and be your husband"—said the doctor, and to toast his plan for the future, he would run into the kitchen where he kept his crates of whisky and he would prepare to steep his body in alcohol, as he did every day. Dalila was taken away on that Carnival morning when the streets were full of adolescents on motorcycles throwing streamers and wearing stupid Carnival masks. The ambulance came and carried him noiselessly away. We were close for a whole decade, but it all happened very fast. Dalila said—"Close the door." His blue car remained parked outside his door for a long time, a long time. A long, long time. Until, after some years had passed, the house of fig trees was sold and they took away Dalila's car. Perhaps in February 1975. I say this so that Walter will know tonight.

62.

Did I say it had been the decade of silence and irony? Yes, I did. In 1974, fifty years late, Alexandrina and Blé suddenly discovered that they had been badly and unfairly treated, in short, oppressed, and they demanded to be given the house at the back where they already lived, remaining exactly where they were, except that they had doors made in the north side in order not to have to meet the former owner. They had no reason to feel grateful to anyone or anything. Fearful that they might, however, they made a point of being rude and unpleasant.

Francisco Dias himself set to working some of the land. Custódio looked after Maria Ema's children. The daughter of Maria Ema and Walter, formerly Walter's niece, found a replacement for Dr. Dalila. Not that one can really speak of replacements, since he had not really taken up much space in her life. It entailed a series of actions identified not by numbers but by faces, which followed each other with the rhythm of those series whose final unit was always breaking down, more like waves than whiskies, for Walter's daughter never put her arms around a lover's neck in order to say—This is the last one. Like waves, like clouds and waves, all of them transient, shifting realities which are unaware they are units in a series, which do not count themselves or say of themselves that they are the last ones. That was why, around 1976, Maria Ema rather missed the peace that had reigned during Dr. Dalila's time. She would sit at the window and watch her daughter setting off very late and say—Please, God, let her find someone as kind as Dr. Dalila. Because Dalila used to live nearby, but now she goes miles away. I knew Dalila, but I don't know who these other men are. I've no sooner found out about one, than along comes another. As long as Dalila was alive, there was only Dalila, and now who knows how many people inhabit the life and body of my daughter. I don't know which towns she goes to or what vices she has. Lord, don't let her turn out like him, the traitor, even though you left a large part of him in her.

Maria Ema was no longer the woman she had been, which was just as well, because it would be unnatural for anyone to remain trapped forever in either good or evil. As for Walter's daughter, she had merely been the heir to a love story of which she knew the preliminaries, the climax and the end, and the knot had unraveled at her feet without anyone dying. The knowledge gained from that was a possession, a credit, a deposit, a solid certainty for her to keep. A legacy. I held that inestimable legacy in my hands.

The truth is that when I used to fall asleep beside Dr. Dalila, I would never dream that I might wake up dead, I always dreamed of being divided. In my dreams, I never died, no one in the family died, we were merely separated, in my dreams.

First, we separated from each other, then from ourselves, then from our limbs, our bellies, our heads, our hands, our fingers. We became transformed into objects, leaves, earth, water, feathers, birdsong, breaking down into trills, mingling with and being borne away by vast stretches of water, until we were no longer part of anything identifiable, we were just sounds. Sounds identical to those made by drops of water, nothing, in the immensity of that infinity of water in which we were absolutely nothing. And the funny thing about those dreams, as I slept on the sofa beside Dr. Dalila, consisted in my being so very far from that initial primeval communion of the two parts of myself and yet still able to remember my beginnings. I was mere divided matter and yet able to remember when I was a person.

Sometimes, Dalila would wake up and, like a contrite king, wander the house in his bathrobe, the belt dragging on the floor, and he would say that the reason I had that dream was because of what he had become. Then he would phone up friends, male and female, who would appear from nowhere, park their cars among the dead leaves and invade the house. He always made sure that one of the male visitors stayed behind to embrace Walter's daughter behind the fridge kept on the landing outside his own bedroom.

63.

But it's not true that I ever said or wrote that the daughter was the result of anything. No, I never said it or wrote it in any letter. To speak of a result, in this case, would be to create the idea of a victim, and Walter's daughter was her own person, and her legacy was a mixture of what she had inherited and the way she herself had transformed that legacy. Walter's daughter would have liked to have been an imitation of the rebel angel who drives the brilliant evening stars and the dark wagons of the night, illuminating the light of others with his own furious darkness. She couldn't be that imitation, but she did not belong to anyone either, she was the fruit of her own person, she was self-born and self-educated. Or so she thought on those happy evenings as she sat with Dr. Dalila. She wrote about it in notebooks adorned with the face of Bob Dylan.

We would sleep on the sofa, under a bedspread, and one day, when she was clearing it of cigarette ashes and ballpoint pens, it suddenly occurred to Walter's daughter to tell him what used to take place on the soldier's blanket. That she had been conceived on the blanket, the same one that served as a seat in the buggy, the same one on which its owner would lie down on the ground in order to make drawings of birds. "A blanket?"—he said. And Dalila started to laugh as only he could laugh. He laughed with a glass in his hand and without, with whisky and without, he laughed until I no longer knew if he was just laughing at that image, to mock the image with which I had so blithely furnished him, or laughing at himself, at Walter's daughter, at heaven and earth and everything else. Then, when he didn't stop laughing, we would both laugh with our arms around each other. We used to get along so well.

I remember this tonight, so that Walter will know.

———

On another occasion, we were sitting in the blue car with our arms about each other, the wheels of the car pointing toward the sea, the high clouds passing slowly overhead, barely moving, and he said—"Isn't it wonderful, all you can hear is the sea." Yes, it was, but human nature rejects Nature's exaggerated bounty, it doesn't trust in its permanence or believe in it as mere simulacrum, and confronted by the regularity of the extravagantly blue sky and sea, by the furious peace born of a raucous beauty, she felt she should do something. Anything to shatter the remarkable, harmonious scene before her, and she remembered a rainy night when she had felt something similar, and she told him about that night. An element of danger undermining the beauty, slicing through that supreme beauty, setting it alight, and, stupidly, idiotically, she mentioned the Smith revolver. Dr. Dalila sat up in his low seat in the blue car to ask her in great alarm—"Do you mean to say that ever since you were a child you've slept with a loaded gun under your mattress? Whose crazy idea was that?" And he sat looking at the landscape which was the same color as his car, only vaster, more liquid, more profound. Otherwise, it was the same dark, intense blue, an angry blue. Then, either because the light was so bright or because of some weakness in his optical nerves, Dr. Dalila, in the middle of that landscape, began to cry. They were small tears that left barely a trace, but they were still visible. They emerged from the corners of his eyes, descended his red cheeks and petered out in his neat beard. Dr. Dalila's beard was always impeccable, unlike his clothes or his car. Walter's daughter turned in her seat and leaned toward him. He said—"If you love me, you'll go home now and fetch that gun and get rid of it. Do you understand? It's the gun or me..." And Dr. Dalila's gaze perused the blue—blue above, blue below, blue on every side. We were an island of flesh in the midst of an almost cloudless lazulite blue. "That's how it is. If a woman needs to sleep each night on top of her father's revolver, it's because she doesn't love her husband. That's how it is. Either you trust me or you don't..." The wet trails of his tears were still there. "Because you know when I do stop drinking once and for all, we'll get married..." Dr. Dalila clearly took the matter very seriously.

Then she waited for the cloud in the south in the form of scattered fish scales, for at least that cloud to move toward the car before they set off for Valmares when it was not quite so light. And so it was. They parked the car some distance from the house; she went in through the kitchen door and grabbed the revolver and the bullets. Then she ran back to Dr. Dalila's car, which set off again at high speed. He glanced at the object in her lap as if at an enemy, talking to it as if it were a man— "Now you're going to get what's coming to you, you son of a bitch!" And he parked the car near a steep slope that gave easy access to the beach. "You stay here"—he said. "And don't move; I'm going to take care of this bastard." And Dr. Dalila, who was, in fact, sober, seemed to be growing gradually drunk. He took off his shoes, waded into the water and with extraordinary fury hurled the Smith revolver into the waves, shouting— "*Requiescat in pace!*" And when he rejoined her, he was drunk as a lord, even though he hadn't touched a drop, not even a swallow of salt water. He kept saying—"You see, you're free now. Why didn't you tell me about it before?" And he asked her to drive the blue car. The blue of late evening, of the encroaching night. I'm only telling all this so that Walter will know.

64.

Later, when she was nearly twenty-five, Walter's daughter concluded that there was no other way of writing phrases like— "*Leave, go, pernicious dream, to the fine ships of the Achaeans*" and she gave herself over to productive tasks, saved some money and bought a Dyane. At night, the headlights of the swaying car would flash briefly across the courtyard wall, sweep past the feet of the black trees and disappear into the darkness. The figure of Maria Ema by the courtyard gate would also vanish rapidly into the shadows and, after a few yards, was nothing. The daughter didn't hang around to find out, but she knew that sometimes Maria Ema would wander in and out of the open doors and across the courtyard, and that Custódio Dias didn't even go to bed. He would walk back and forth, up and down the road, until the headlights of the Dyane announced her return home. Then he would stop and, although he was never exactly agile, he would nevertheless manage to leap like a hare out of the road and hide among the agaves so that he wouldn't be seen. But if they did meet, the daughter did not slow down or flash her lights at him if she saw him by the road. He could go home the way he had come, stumbling through the grass, following the ruts left by the car, with the asymmetrical gait of the lame. She wasn't grateful to him for the ambulatory watch he kept, she had never asked them to stand guard over her.

It was almost as if Maria Ema had read the same solemn ancient texts her daughter read. In them, divine forces played with men, and Fate looked on appreciatively, as she should. Maria Ema would shout after her daughter, waving her two arms in the air—"Who is it that calls to you in the night, you wicked girl? Another drunkard?" Maria Ema suffered. Her daughter never said as much to Maria Ema, but it was true. Around 1976, she knows perfectly well who it is that calls to her. She is called by the drunkard, by the red-faced old man with a scar on his head and one eye closed, with teeth missing on one side, a broken nose and a knife hidden in one sock, by the man who killed his wife, who smells of mice, who stinks of whisky, whose sweat reeks, who brooks no disagreement, who shouts rather than talks, who is too lazy to get out of bed, who never keeps his word, who sprains his wrist so that he can't work, who refuses to get up, who has no job, who doesn't want a job, who drifts, who arrives on a boat and leaves in a meat truck amidst the slabs of meat, who's always expecting a visit from the police, who crushes the petals of lilies, who spits out chewed grass and uses a toothpick. The man with the hairy body, whose gaze is lecherous, who has sloughed off his soul, who causes accidents, who never studied mathematics, who thinks Homer is the name of a dog, who is not presentable and is invisible in the light of day or even by the light of the moon, who only takes shape in the dark of the night. That is the disgusting creature who squeezes her fingers, nuzzles her nipple, sucks her toe. But she never says that. She writes it.

Twenty-six.

They were arguing in front of Francisco Dias. The daughter had just driven up in the Dyane and was screaming at her mother that she was invulnerable. "Invulnerable?"—Maria Ema was screaming back. "And what kind of word is that, may I ask?" The daughter was saying—"Yes, invulnerable!" What she meant, during that argument, was that her soul had always been invulnerable, her soul, that niche in which she curls up and hides, where she spends the nights, where she knows what she knows and does not yet know how much more there still is not to know. And that is why it suited her that the person squeezing her nipple, touching the nape of her neck, dragging her by the hair to the broken-backed mattresses of vacation homes, should be so banal, so trivial, so gross, that they do not even get near the entrance to the hiding place where her soul is to be found, wrapped in its vestments of silk. That was her private domain, her legacy, her royal park where only she could hunt, where only she could loose her dogs and catch her antlered deer. All this was incomprehensible to Maria Ema and to Custódio Dias, who was both her uncle and her father, and especially to Francisco Dias, the perplexed loser of arable lands. Francisco Dias would shout to Custódio Dias when he stood watching for the Dyane at the end of the road, while Maria Ema waited in the courtyard—"Let her go! I hope she goes and never comes back. I hope she stays there for good and leaves us in peace." It was the summer of 1978. And meanwhile Maria Ema began to relinquish her grandiose manner of calling on God. "What's the point, if He neither hears me nor sees her?"—she asked.

65.

Yes, it was the decade of silence. But whenever she wanted him to, Walter would take off his shoes, and, holding them in one hand, appear at her door as he had on that rainy night. He didn't knock, he didn't need to, the door was always ready to be entered and she knew it. The oil lamp lit the shoulders of his raincoat, there was no need to raise it to eye level. Walter walked about the room, went over to the wardrobe and even to the table with the books on it, without saying a word, he just came and went. He placed a hand on her belongings, he agreed with what she had to say, they discussed things rather than argued. Sometimes they laughed. We understood each other, we were more than contented, we were happy. I no longer had the gun in the room, but it didn't matter if it was there or not. Wherever it was, on the surface of the sand or being buried deeper and deeper each passing second beneath the pounding waves where Dr. Dalila had thrown it, the Smith revolver had served its purpose. Not even the album of birds or what remained of the films was essential now. The important thing in that time of silence is that whenever she called him, he came, he would come up the stairs and appear at the door as on that night in 1963.

———

Francisco Dias did not sleep either, but for a very different reason. His insomnia came from another kind of silence.

It was the silence of the Dias brothers. He would get up in the night, convinced that his sons' failure to give a date for their return was the most palpable sign that they were about to come back. When sunset approached, he would ask Custódio to leave the iron gate to the courtyard ajar in case they came back and couldn't get in. He didn't know whether they would come by train or taxi, as Walter had years before. He thought, though, that the first hypothesis was the most likely one, because his other sons were not spendthrifts or wastrels. Unless, of course, they came back in their own cars, and if that should be the case, there would be two families per car, to make traveling cheaper. Six families in three cars. However they did it, they were bound to return. The arguments for their prompt return lay in the hills around and in the house itself. Besides, everyone came back, why wouldn't the Dias brothers?

The truth was that, with each hour that passed, the arguments piled up around the house. He would hold up his right hand and number them on his fingers—The Dias boys were about to arrive because in Valmares the explosions in the quarries caused continual earth tremors, opening up cracks in the walls as big as your arm, and the dust fell on the roof and filtered down into their beds like flour. The birds from the mudflats, fleeing the earthmoving work near the dunes, turned up in large, disoriented flocks in the dried stubble fields, laying their eggs out of season and in the wrong places. Certain weeds disappeared, while other unknown varieties proliferated. The ripening figs split into nine segments, the green olives remained black and thin for lack of rain. The earth was so dry. He watched the wind lifting the earth into the air and carrying it off to other places, he watched the arable soil growing thin and skeletal. Standing on the hill, he saw what no one else saw—the earth rising into the air like a cloud of smoke borne on the wind. It seemed to him that, starting with his own world, the world itself was breaking up, shriveling and dying. He wanted his sons to return in order to set right something much larger than his own house. And when they did come, even if they were not as rich as they had hoped to be, it would be in order to reclaim the land that belonged to them, to anchor the earth with trees and other plants. Then, in her room, Walter's daughter, occasionally accompanied by people who spoke other languages, whom she met on other roads, would hear Francisco go outside in the early hours of the morning to groom the last mule. She would listen—He didn't want to let that last animal go, he didn't want to break the last animal link that bound him to the work that had made the money that had built the house. In the morning, he would wash, get dressed and harness the mule and go and stand in the middle of the courtyard, his arms folded. Unlike his granddaughter, he was still waiting.

66.

Besides, in the mid-seventies, Francisco Dias cannot accept that changes so opposed to his view of life can possibly have taken place, changes that impinge on the very meaning of his past life and on his deepest hopes, and that his children do not want to help him. As he waits by the gate, which stands wide open, melancholy immobilizes him. He doesn't understand how the sons of those to whom he once gave work, those who came to him with downcast eyes, who thanked him over and over when he advanced them ten escudos, or paid them for the whole day if they were overcome by pain during their work and had to lie down in the fields, those same men now sit at their front doors doing nothing, and their sons buy up lands, businesses and houses as if they were wealthy men. Instead of him enlarging his territory as he had planned, the sons of his workers share borders with him, threaten his cherished but deferred ambitions, asking him to sell or, on the contrary, telling him they're not interested in anything he has to offer. In the mid-seventies, the owner of Valmares is a very troubled farmer, the work on his farm constantly postponed because his sons have still not come home. He cannot wait any longer. They'll pay for it. They'll pay.

Francisco utters these threats out loud, he wants to leave too, to get on a plane for the first time in his life and go and find them. He wants to tell them off, to call them traitors, the same or worse than Walter. He walks around the house at night, he packs various belongings and clothes into a bag, counts out money on his bed, does calculations in his head, goes to Faro to buy a new felt hat of a sort no longer made. He tries to catch the mail train as he used to in the days when he went to the cattle market, and wants to keep his money in his hat just as his father did before him. In short, he wants to set off on that great journey of confrontation with his sons. He tears the map of the world off the wall and folds it up small to fit in his wallet, so that he can get it out when he arrives and go in search of his sons and slap them across the face as he used to do when they were boys. He puts a handkerchief in his pocket and a penknife in his sock. There he goes down the road, dragging his bags and suitcases with him. During the summer months of 1975, Custódio will spend those unforgettable, hot nights bringing him back home. Things are getting serious in Valmares.

67.

The problem was Valmares itself. I can still hear the international phone calls Custódio made to his brothers. Walter's daughter finds it odd they should be at home to answer the phone, because she always imagines them journeying to the West through inhospitable landscapes, trailing their wives behind them and producing children, a few children, all alike, at least according to the photos they send, far, far away in the land they will have settled in. But now, worried about Francisco Dias, who is in a permanent state of anxiety, sitting by the door beside his suitcases, Custódio tracks each one down across those cosmic distances and talks to them from the entrance hall, telling them their return is now a matter of urgency. Custódio explains that he's losing patience, it's vital they reach some agreement, that they phone back soon. Their father has finally realized that they have their own lives far away, too far away, and now he feels hurt that they don't want to come home, not even to divide up the house.

At the other end, they say they understand perfectly. But they don't phone back, they just send letters. Short letters. They seem to come from people extraordinarily like the silent images of those men she sees amalgamated into a kind of work brigade, silently laboring away among the animals in the courtyard in the mid-fifties. She cannot remember each individual face, only their names, ages and attributes, the year when they left and the first letters they wrote. Maria Ema would say to Custódio Dias—"I bet you she could persuade them to come and sort this out just by writing them a few nicely worded letters. Go on, ask her, please." She meant Walter's daughter.

She was wrong, though.

Walter's daughter cannot write to people whom she keeps frozen in her memory. She knows nothing about their subsequent lives, she has difficulty attributing separate destinies to them all, apart from those described in their first letters, but those are fixed in time and she wants to keep them like that. It makes perfect sense that they should still be there, disappearing as they did years ago, elusive and distant. One of them still walks across a white blanket of snow, dragging tree trunks, he continues to labor on that snowy surface, running after a truck onto which he has to throw the logs, struggling to keep pace with the truck, which does not stop. She still sees him following the tire tracks in the snow, she sees him disappearing into the tall trees, into the dark shadows, Joaquim Dias, working as a lumberjack in the flat lands of Nova Scotia. The film she has of him is stuck there, and she cannot wind it forward or back. She can see the one who worked down in the mines too, the one in the photo wearing a lamp on his hat, a tin hat, the sweat pouring off him, in the depths of the earth, at the coal face, it's dark, she can barely make him out. She sees him filling a bucket with bits of rock. It is Manuel Dias, one of the first to leave. She can hear his slightly hoarse voice, as if he were still standing outside the house in Valmares, but his voice is reverberating dully in the depths of the earth, underneath Elliot Lake. How can they possibly come back?

68.

Regardless of whether they turn out to be the same or utterly different, she doesn't want them back. She wants them to remain as she created and maintained them during the time she lived with Dr. Dalila. She enjoys the image of the one who used to knock down houses. That was Luís Dias. He had abandoned Francisco Dias' scything to go and demolish wooden walls. In the seventies, she could still hear the dry, hollow sound of Luís Dias' mallet smashing through windows, doors, roofs, leaving behind him a trail of houses transformed into heaps of planks and piled-up windows, in the shade of the maple trees. "This is a maple tree"—he wrote on the back of a photograph sent in the fifties. But the most interesting of them all was the one in the United States, standing in the middle of an endless plain in which the only features on the otherwise smooth earth were the backs of the cattle. He was João Dias, with a stick in his hand, in the middle of a plain, as if he were standing guard by day over a starry night turned inside out. Franciso Dias had not even wanted to look at it. How could a wealthy man's son be a mere cattle herder, in charge of those slow beasts, in a place devoid of houses? It was a lovely photograph. João Dias should stay there alone in the middle of the plain, with only a man from the Azores for company, leading the languid cows into the pen.

But the unbearably beautiful image which, over the years, had always awoken in her a feeling of fierce joy belonged to Fernandes, Adelina's husband, the one who had taught her how to write the W of Walter on an afternoon when the chickens were still pecking in the yard. In the seventies, she can see him struggling to write, his fingers worn almost to the bone. He was the one who worked for the railway company, for Canadian Pacific. I can see him leaving that bloody fingerprint on the paper and the explanation read out to us by Adelina—*Forgive me, Adelina, I didn't want to send you this letter, but I haven't got any more paper or ink here, and I need to send you news of me today. I don't know what else to do* . . . And then the photograph of Fernandes in the middle of the broken ballast, a railway sleeper on his shoulder. She would always imagine him laying a line of iron across Canada, between Ontario and Alberta and British Columbia, heading west. In that image, he was placing his hand on that line of iron and the train was running over his arm. On the other side, in the form of an outstretched hand, lay Canada.

The image was too shocking to bear, but she had borne it for years, as a revenge on Francisco Dias.

The one in Caracas offered Walter's daughter the least clear image. The letter it was based on was incomplete, but even after all this time, she still imagined him hungry. She remembers him writing that he used to pick up fruit from the ground to fill his stomach, and that, out of respect for the name of his father, the farmer, he had preferred not to get covered in flour or to deliver bread door-to-door on a bicycle. He used to eat a fruit similar to an orange, but smooth and green outside and with just one seed and no sections. It was delicious, even though his reasons for eating it were sad. But when Inácio had written describing how he had resisted entering the bakery business, he was already working on a building site beneath a crane. She had no concrete image, either good or bad. She could not see him, or, rather, he formed part of the collective, growing ever more abstract and remote, fixed as he was twenty years before, according to those early letters, read out loud by their wives and by Custódio Dias. And, of course, later, the person who really mattered had come, Walter had come, eclipsing everything and everyone, mixing up all the Dias brothers and transforming them into one shapeless mass, reducing them to a single insignificant face. She could not remember the others. Why was Custódio asking her to make such an effort of memory?

69.

But then, why waste time hoping they wouldn't come back? You could tell from their letters that they wouldn't. Why bother answering them? At a time when distances meant nothing and traveling had become so banal that one could get on a plane in the clothes one wore around the house or did the gardening in, it seemed that the Dias brothers did not want to visit their father, but they didn't say so outright, they kept putting off a decision they should have taken ages ago, and then they would write neat letters full of sly excuses. I say this tonight, sitting before Walter's soldier's blanket, so that Walter will know.

The letters that reached Valmares and were delivered to the São Sebastião post office were wise letters, letters that concealed what should be concealed and that spoke only of what could be spoken of. Measured letters with each word weighed, each sentence honed. Unlike other emigrants from Valmares, who wrote poignant letters full of nostalgia and made phone calls that must have cost as much as an airplane ticket, and who occasionally paid rowdy visits that seemed to give them the strength to go on and to be their real reason for living, the Dias brothers felt comfortable at a distance and did not want to come back. Those letters, I remember, always began the same way. You can tell a mile off that they don't miss Valmares at all. More than that, they must dread having to divide up among them the empire of stones that Francisco Dias' house has become.

They must want to avoid the drama, the discord, the hysteria involved in sharing out a legacy of nothing and for nothing. The absent Dias brothers are willing to pay in order to have nothing, so as not to inherit piles of stones, scrubby fields, sandy, chalky lands that no one wants to plant or build on or do anything with. Between the sea and the mountains, their father created an empire out of a worthless bit of land, not realizing he would end up a king of stones. Indeed, each night, the stones roll down from the walls he had had built decades before. Among them the scrubby trees bloom as if neglect were a vitamin and scorn the best possible manure, as if they grew in order not to be seen. Only the king of those scrublands has failed to realize that they dominate his territory. The Dias brothers, scattered throughout the Americas, do not want the bother of that grim legacy, of those fields rapidly reverting to type—arid lands which are the natural habitat of desolation, the genet and the fox. The Dias brothers will never come back. Walter's daughter could guess as much from the letters she only half-listened to, they didn't have time, didn't have enough vacation. But Francisco Dias would pace around outside, go up to the main door, fling it open and, before Walter's daughter left in the Dyane, he would shout to Custódio—"Go on, be brave! Kick her out of the house!"

70.

Walter's daughter did occasionally have time and, without Custódio's telling her to, she did occasionally write letters describing the king of the scrublands and would cautiously await a response. But their letters did not change. They were delaying letters, sly letters of disengagement, that offered no possible practical outcome. And then, toward the end of the seventies, the Dias brothers suddenly open up a parenthesis to discuss a subject that should never have been mentioned. Stubborn and circumspect, motivated by cunning, they all began writing about something that had long been kept silent and stored away, and that should never have been discussed. They began writing about Walter, about Walter's untouchable image. I accuse the Dias brothers of trying, through those letters, to destroy the legacy left to Walter Dias' daughter.

I recall those letters, separated by months and years, in their implacably coherent whole, so that Walter will know of them tonight. I call to them, unfold them, reread them. They have their own order. They arrange themselves by date, they select themselves, memory purifies and smooths them, burns out any superfluous descriptions, the repetitive words of greeting, and joins them together like the segments on an endless caterpillar. Their theme is the following—The only member of the family whom the Dias brothers believe to be in a position to return and take over Valmares is Walter. As far as they can see, their brother continues to wander from city to city as once he sailed from port to port. Unlike them, he has no fixed business or permanent abode. Walter is the only one who is free, who has not put down roots or established a legal family in any of the cities he has lived in. That is why he is the only one who could return with the urgency Custódio requires. Anyway, it would be a good opportunity for Walter to put into practice what he had mentioned to his father in 1963, scaring the life out of him. They knew that Walter had worried their father with the idea of selling the house. Well, now was his chance to go back and deal with that serious matter. Yes, he should go back. But where was Walter? He had to be found. And then, from images constructed twenty years before, the Dias brothers begin to emerge out of the distance, with new faces, precise names and spouses, individual lives and recent, real addresses, shattering and churning up the residual world of Valmares.

71.

It turns out that Fernandes, he of the unbearably beautiful image she had created of him on a railway line, owns a real estate office in Vancouver. Joaquim Dias, the lumberjack running in the snow, has become a maker of garden benches with a workshop in Halifax. His letters are written on headed notepaper. The miner, Manuel Dias, owns a limousine service in Ottawa. Luís Dias introduces himself as a builder, and João Dias shares not only a few languid cows with his Azorean colleague, but also a large commercial dairy. And Inácio? Inácio has his own construction business—La Constructora Ideal. He builds houses, buildings, tall apartment blocks. Palpable, diverse and real, the Dias brothers had transformed themselves into a universal family. Francisco Dias' universal sons finally give some account of their lives. They do so in order to be able to talk about Walter. Maria Ema reads the letters. She can read. She says that Walter Dias means nothing to her. She even goes on to say that she will only be happy when he has disappeared from the face of the earth, or the face of the sea, which is where she always imagines him, moving ever farther off, borne along on the sheer immensity of the sea.

Anyway, this seems to be a time when nothing happens beyond those letters, when everything stops. The wind stops, the waves stop. Tonight I evoke that paralysis in order to remember those unforgettable letters. So that Walter will know.

The first is written by Vitória, the wife of the one with the limousine service, Manuel Dias, who had once been a miner with a special lamp attached to his helmet. Frugal when it comes to facts about her own family, Manuel's wife merely says that in Ottawa it occasionally gets dark too early, but that otherwise everything is fine. Their children study and play the saxophone, and Manuel was made president of a club. But, naturally, she is writing for another reason.

She is writing to say her husband agrees that Walter should be found, that Walter should return to their father's house in order to sort out the inheritance, because, apart from anything else, she fears that her brother-in-law, wherever he is, may not be well. Years ago, he had a travel agency right by the lake, on Harbor Street. Walter's travel agency arranged trips, drew up contracts, translated documents, acted as an agent for lawyers, Walter was respected. Until he got a young girl pregnant and fled across the snow. The last time a fellow Portuguese immigrant had seen him, he was heading for the Falls. They had met by chance in a roadside restaurant. He was traveling in a black car, with half a dozen suitcases, one of them on the roof rack. He had disappeared.

And, she added–Fortunately, the young girl was from a Polish family. If she had been the daughter of Italians, they would have killed him by now. But not Poles. They're patient people. The girl had already had an affair with someone else. Now she had had two affairs and a baby. And the baby was a boy. But Walter had left without bothering about the child. He had abandoned the travel agency, leaving important matters unresolved and, on the wall, pictures of wild geese drawn by him—And after that, we never heard from him again, it must be six years now. Custódio should try the embassies. Someone will find him and tell him to go back to Valmares–*From Vitória and Manuel Dias, Limo Service, Ottawa.*

72.

I remember hearing that letter read out. Maria Ema, sitting up very straight, had put it down on the table, laughing at the reference to the Polish girl. Custódio couldn't believe it– "It's incredible. Six years have gone by, and they've never once mentioned that child, that little boy…" Francisco Dias asked them not to read any more, Walter would never change. Would they please just skip a few lines whenever they saw the word "Walter."

But after a week and a half, a letter from João Dias provided another clue. Francisco Dias' sixth son also wrote a circular letter to all the members of the family. It came from that broad, timeless plain like an inverted sky, with cows scattered as far as the horizon, from inside a dairy plant, with its tanks for sterilization, pasteurization, skimming, for producing cream and butter, a soft, white, creamy, industrial wealth, he emerged from all that in order to talk about Walter, although he didn't have much time to devote to writing such letters.

He came straight to the point—Between the San Joaquin valley where they lived and the East Coast where Walter lived, it was a solid six-hour flight. Four or five years before, on a weekend, they had gone to visit their brother, who was doing well at the time and didn't need to work very hard because he was running a very successful jewelry business. Although they didn't need anything, since the dairy farm they owned provided them with everything, Walter, who did not live quite as well as they did, had insisted on paying all their expenses, including the hotel, which was proof he was still not used to how much things cost in the States. He had insisted, saying it was a token of his affection for them, but João and his wife both felt it was sheer extravagance. Apart from that, they had gone with him to a bay so as to see something of the coast, and Walter, sitting at the window of a restaurant built of wood, had found time to draw some birds, some lovely drawings which he had left behind there. The point was that, a week later, when they had phoned to thank him, the phone had been cut off at both Theodhoros & Walter, Jewelers and at his house.

In short, João Dias and his wife, Teresa, saw no point in going looking for a man like that in order to put the Valmares house in order—*From Jo Dias, San Joaquin.*

It really wasn't worth it. Anyway, it never had been, even

though the idea had come from them, not from Custódio or Francisco Dias. So why waste time unsaying what they had said? But the letters had only just begun.

73.

Shortly afterward, Adelina wrote from Vancouver. The correspondence had gathered dust in a drawer in São Sebastião de Valmares for a fortnight because no one could be bothered to deliver the mail by bike anymore. Custódio collected it and read it that night, standing by the table. It was a letter that was both informative and inspired. Adelina's husband, the man with the bloody fingerprint who had long since left the railway lines of the Canadian Pacific and no longer had his face covered in dust from the ballast or his nails torn off from lifting sleepers. The unbearable image of endless beauty had died. Fernandes, Adelina's husband, had been buying and selling houses for some years now. The same finger that had once left bloodstains on letters now wrote numbers on checks without leaving a single fingerprint. And it turned out that, whether buying or selling, Fernandes was always lucky because the prices were always in his favor. "Speaking of sales, I must tell you about Walter"—Adelina wrote.

Speaking of buying and selling houses, we've had some news of Walter. Four years ago, he closed the jeweler's shop he half-owned with a Greek fellow in Providence. He just disappeared between one day and the next. The Greek was left with the business and with all the capital to manage. Apparently, the Greek even had the river dragged for Walter's body and for his car, but they never found anything. A young man over from Massachusetts to buy a house in Vancouver had told them this. As I said, Adelina went on, we're always very busy, but we're happy here. Lovely flowers bloom in the snow, as if they had opened up beneath the earth and only appeared on the surface when they could make a full bouquet. As clean and tidy as if the bulbs were growing in pots. Here, even the cemeteries are green and fertile. People go for walks among the graves with their children and grandchildren and they're not afraid. For them the dead are as alive as we are, which is why they're quite happy strolling through graveyards. Here. Otherwise, we have no news to give you about Walter. Wrote Adelina. And only then did she close the letter—*From Adelina and José Fernandes, Real Estate Broker, Vancouver.*

74.

Francisco Dias didn't want to hear any more. "Just skip any sentence where you see the W of Walter!" But that wasn't possible. The letters from the Dias family, almost entirely written in Portuguese, as if when they wrote to Valmares they wanted to avoid leaving any trace of the languages in which they lived immersed, spoke only of Walter. "All right, read it then"—Francisco Dias would say, leaning on the table.

Yes, after two months, from the post office in São Sebastião de Valmares, comes another circular letter from Caracas. It's from Luísa, wife and business partner of Inácio Dias, who writes from the La Carlota district of Caracas. Luísa is replying, on behalf of her husband, to Custódio's appeals for them to come back and share out among them all those fields of sand and stones. Inácio Dias, alas, cannot leave his business even for a day. Luísa writes of an impending crisis in the building industry. A crisis that affects the building of houses, mansions, even skyscrapers. Inácio doesn't have time even to write a letter, let alone make a journey to sort out the complicated Dias inheritance. And then Luísa, very excited, mentions Walter—"In case you don't know where Walter is, hold on to your hats, because you're in for a surprise—Walter's living in Caracas."

She can't understand the rumor about his having been drowned in Narragansett Bay, when everyone knows he's been living in Venezuela for the last year and a half–He arrived and didn't get in touch with anyone, not even Inácio. We met him after he'd become a partner in a jewelry business. We found out, though, that when he came here from the United States, he started out working in a sawmill and that, for the first six months, he slept in his car under the mango trees. He only looked us up a year later, when he had the jewelry store, though that's no big deal in this part of town. That's why, as regards persuading him to go back to Valmares and take charge of Pa's land, we're all in favor. If the crisis affects building, it's bound to affect luxuries like gold and silver. He's starting to show his age too, though he still looks very presentable, he's always well-dressed and drives a sharp car. But everyone knows about him here. And Luísa started a new paragraph.

They say that when he's had too much to drink, he gets

out a blanket and puts it around his shoulders and sings. They also say that he spreads it out on the bed when he wants to have sex with a woman. Inácio says it's the blanket he had when he did his military service. They say he goes to the El Silencio district in Caracas and waves his blanket at the girls. Our name is being associated with some most unfortunate rumors. We're very much afraid his reputation will in some way harm our children, who are studying law and sociology. Who would dream of using an old army blanket as a sheet? In the Portuguese community, they say he came from the States where he laid women down on his blanket and then abandoned the children he made there. That's what they say. We'll write to Pa today to tell Custódio to write Walter and ask him to go back there, because he's bringing shame on our name and on Portugal. The people here are very patriotic. That's why Inácio told me to make six copies of this letter and send one to each of his brothers. With best wishes—*Luísa and Inácio Dias, La Constructora Ideal, Caracas.*

75.

Then the letters began coming thick and fast. There was barely a line that did not contain some comment about Walter. In the archaic post office of São Sebastião de Valmares, there are sometimes two letters in the same drawer. A kind of fuse has been lit between the Americas and São Sebastião de Valmares, as if the three continents were no longer separated by the undulating mass of the Atlantic. In 1981, the letters cross each other, many of them are registered and have to be signed for. I reread those letters, I cannot remember anything else that happened in between. They occupy that entire period, a strange time, like the moment filled by a flash of lightning. I can't remember anything else apart from what is written in them. I lean over the letters, as if over a body in the process of being poisoned. The first one to arrive, after Luísa had written to tell us where Walter was, is a letter from Vancouver. A poisoned letter.

"Pa!"—the letter began, as if the sender were talking not writing. Over there in her house in Vancouver, Adelina, the one who received the bloodstained letter from her husband, suddenly remembers everything, now she's been reminded about the blanket.

She dismisses the Narragansett Bay episode and goes back to 1951 and recalls how when Walter came back as a quartermaster from India, he got rid of everything he owned, apart from that blanket, the same blanket on which he slept with the girls from Valmares. "Do you remember, Pa?" Adelina Dias has a talent for telling stories and for writing. At that point, the handwriting improves and the syntax speeds up. Adelina deftly explains that a soldier's blanket is holy ground. A blanket is the symbol of the hard military life, and she says that her brother destroyed that symbol and diverted it from its normal course. He transformed the blanket into an ugly flag, a rather frightening flag when viewed from another country.

She knows that Walter wandered around India, went from India to Australia, from Australia to Africa, and then, for six years, wandered from port to port between the two Atlantic coasts. The blanket bears traces of earth from all those places. It must be stained with brine, with muddy earth, with fertile earth, with earth full of creepy-crawlies from the coasts of Africa, with mosquito-ridden earth from Central America, and the frozen snow waters of Ontario must have blurred all those stains into one; that blanket of his was a veritable atlas. Recalling the past, she is in a position to say that Walter does not use the blanket to sit on when he's drawing birds. He uses that soldier's blanket to lie down on to rest, or to "work" in the disgusting sense we're all too familiar with. And before closing, she adds—"Pa, by now, we must have relatives scattered all around the world, with his eyes, with Walter's eyes, which are sometimes like a cheetah's eyes and sometimes like a cat's. Walter's tawny eyes…" Then Adelina added a few words apologizing for everything, then, lots of love from—*Adelina and José Fernandes, Real Estate Broker, Vancouver.*

Yes, it was a poisoned letter. I remember those letters from Adelina. It's a baking hot April afternoon, the trees are casting solitary shadows on the flagstones. The three of them are sitting in the courtyard. Maria Ema isn't reading, she's listening. Custódio won't read out everything, because of his father, he says. But she asks him to read it all, she wants to know what happened to Walter in the past. She finds it interesting and asks him to read that letter from Vancouver from the first line to the last. "Good grief, Walter's life has become a real circus! Read it again!"—she said as if it had nothing at all to do with her, as if she were someone else. She herself reads it for a third time, standing by the table. Sometimes she falls asleep at the table with the letters beside her, and with her glasses on, the frame of her glasses pressed against the pages of the letters.

76.

Then, from far away, Teresa, João Dias' wife, the dairywoman, rebels. Years ago, she had visited Walter's city, with all expenses paid by him, but now she must speak the truth. Now, when she remembers her brother-in-law drawing birds beside that bay, she could swear he was sitting on that blanket.

She can clearly remember that, after a meal during which he had sketched a few of the birds flying about, he had gone to get a blanket out of the trunk of his car and sat down on it, spread it out over the seawall, and that she had found it amusing, though João was furious. But now she knew the blanket had had other uses. And both she and her husband, emerging from the churns of cream and the kiloliters of pasteurized milk, stand firmly foursquare by the customs of the flat land they live in, a land of purity, decency and honor, a land as clean as the prairie itself, to speak out on behalf of decency—Here, the flag is not just an object, it is sacred. Everyone worships the flag. Most families fly it at their front door or from the roof. On Fridays, even the drunks sing holding the flag, and not even drink gives them the right to dishonor such a symbol. Americans give their lives for their country which, as they themselves say, is more than just America, it is Democracy itself. That is why it would never occur to an American soldier no matter how old, no matter how bohemian, to use a soldier's blanket for such things, such awful things! And so Teresa and the dairyman João Dias advise against recalling Walter to take care of his father's land in Valmares. And in the last lines, the couple withdrew into all that butter and milk, into the udders of their two thousand cows. Mingling the lives of the cows with their children's auspicious lives, all of whom were well and all with good jobs—*From Teresa and Jo Dias, San Joaquin.*

"That's it!"—Francisco Dias had said, sitting in the shade cast by the trees and the wall. "I don't want to hear any more of those foul letters, I'm not interested in what they have to say. Instead of wasting their time spreading accusations, they could be over here doing their duty. But, oh no, they won't do that." And pacing up and down in the courtyard like an old corralled animal, he said his children were having fun at his expense, their own father, they were copying Walter's tricks. "Calm down, Pa!"—Custódio said, reading the letter out loud again for Maria Ema to hear.

As I said, they were poisoned letters.

77.

As it happens, it was Manuel Dias himself, the one who had been a miner, who replied to Francisco Dias, to Custódio and to Maria Ema, having first replied to Inácio, the one in South America. In a very long, solemn letter, he reminded us that, in his journey through that land, he had progressed from the darkest depths of the earth to the most select part of downtown

Ottawa, where he owned a wonderful car rental firm, which also offered the use of six taxis and two limousines, and to achieve that, it had been necessary to suffer a great deal, to learn a great deal and to distrust a lot of people, which had not been easy. But Walter, now in his fifties, seemed unaware of the necessity of making any real effort, and was still drawing birds and bedding women on that wretched soldier's blanket of his. He didn't even want to mention the vile thing. He was only writing to say what he had said in his letter to Inácio Dias, that it was always hard to say when Walter's being around was a good or a bad thing. Because, there was no doubt about it, Walter went through different phases. And just so that his father and brothers and sister knew, he was going to reveal what had long remained hidden—For a time, when Walter had been working as travel agent cum translator cum legal go-between, Walter had helped him out. He had helped him a lot and never taken any money. But later, when he traveled to Valmares in 1963, Walter had borrowed money from him to buy the car he drove to show off in front of his father and the rest of the family, and he had never paid him back. So, a large part of the car in which they had traveled during that visit had come out of Manuel Dias' pocket. The Chevrolet that had provided the backdrop to the photographs Walter had taken of his nephews and niece had been paid for by the sweat of Manuel's brow and the frugality of his good wife. He felt, therefore, that one could never quite know what to expect from Walter. At that precise moment, Walter owed him more than five thousand dollars with interest. He felt they should know that—*From Manuel Dias, Limo Service, Ottawa.*

That letter from Manuel Dias was read about twenty times. We read it and read it, almost breathlessly, in the middle of the courtyard surrounded by the shadows of the trees. "He conned us..."—said Custódio for the first time. "All the time we were in that car, he was conning us...It wasn't really his."

No, it wasn't his. Maria Ema read and reread the passages regarding the debt, unable to interpret what she was reading. Was the car really not his? Irritated by those letters describing earthly realities totally alien to him, Francisco Dias unexpectedly spoke out in support of Walter—"Doesn't the work Walter did for him count, then? Maybe the one who's making these accusations has wronged Walter, just as he's wronged me too. Oh, they're all the same..."

Whatever the truth of the matter, after that letter from Ottawa, the fact that Walter had driven his father, his brother and sister-in-law and their children around in a car paid for by someone else became central to the memories surrounding Francisco Dias' youngest son. The three of them seemed not to want to believe it. The images they had stored away, and that were still there in various forms in the coffers of their lives, must have left some trace of beauty there, how else could one understand the shock they felt when they read those lines for the twenty-second time. If the images were now sullied, it was because, before, each of those bright, smooth images had survived in them, just as they had in his daughter. Walks, drives, surprises, all in the grip of a power we had imagined in 1963 and kept in precious places inside our heads, like living creatures still intact despite the passing of time, all these were murdered by that letter from Manuel Dias, the one whose harsh voice we used to hear talking in the courtyard. As she held the letter in her hands, Maria Ema suddenly looked like an old woman. When she read it yet again, her neck folded like a wing. Her back became a buttress supporting her sunken chest. Her face was lined, her hair gray. Her ankles swollen. Of course, that deterioration had been happening gradually, time had slowly been working away without anyone's noticing, but it was only then that Walter's daughter noticed how Maria Ema had changed. She would take off her reading glasses and say to Custódio—"It was all a lie, nothing he came here to do was true..." Her husband, looking up at the tops of the waterless trees, would say—"Yes, I know..." Late April 1981.

And then, with barely a pause, another letter would arrive confirming the last one, or in some way related to it. They were quick to open it. It was from Luís Dias, who had spent twenty years locked in the same image, demolishing wooden houses, resting by a maple tree, and who was now a builder in Hamilton, and he said—I read Manuel's letter, and I certainly wouldn't have put up with that! We must do something to help Luísa and Inácio before Walter cons them too. Not to mention the blanket. Can you imagine the state it must be in. Just the thought of the disgusting thing makes me ashamed to be a Dias. In the world we live in in the Americas, it only takes one bad apple to ruin a family's reputation—*From Luís Dias, Hamilton.* They folded the letter.

"They all agree"—Maria Ema would say, standing by the door, her head resting on her husband's shoulder. "They certainly seem to"—Custódio Dias would stay, stroking her loose, gray hair, which now she pinned back on one side only.

78.

It was true. Valmares seemed to have become a warehouse through which those circular letters passed, and no sooner had one arrived than it was followed by another, typewritten letter from Halifax. It was from Joaquim Dias. A brief letter. The inventive maker of garden seats, remembering the times when he used to load timber onto trucks, wrote these few warning lines—"I take no responsibility for any debts incurred by Walter Dias in the United States of America, in any other part of North or South America, or in Portugal or any other part of the world"—*Signed by my own hand, Joaquim Dias. Woodcraft, Halifax.*

Custódio didn't have to write a single line of reply to get other responses. Now the Dias family were corresponding among themselves like a close family with a mail center in Valmares.

The next letter was truly shocking.

"Dear Father-in-law, dear brother and dear sister-in-law"— wrote Luísa, without Custódio's ever having written to her. We are very worried. Walter has left the jewelry business he was running. He has disappeared. The shop is shut and the house all closed up. The parking place where he used to leave his car is now occupied by someone else. What is Inácio supposed to think? That perhaps the business wasn't legal? You can never be too sure when it comes to gold and silver and precious stones, especially when you're dealing with a man who spent six years on board ship, traveling from port to port. How did he make his money? Deep-sea fishing? Drawing birds? He obviously did make money, enough to start up and later close down all those different businesses, doubtless illicitly. Some people say he was traveling on a suspicious boat, under a Liberian flag, which is the worst there is. We don't know—"Whatever the truth of the matter, may God forgive us if we're being unfair, but, as you can well understand, we're both very worried." And then the wife of Inácio Dias, who, in the far-off fifties, had turned down jobs in the baking world and had sent a photo of himself working under a crane, gave a detailed account of the crisis that kept husband, children and herself tied to a fertile land on which they were putting up buildings as fast as they could, though why they didn't know. "So we won't be coming to Portugal for quite some time. And we're very sorry to give you the news about Walter"—*Luísa and Inácio Dias, La Constructora Ideal, Caracas.*

Maria Ema and Custódio no longer slept in the west room; they occupied one near the living room, in the middle of the house. She would wake up early thinking about the post office's irregular opening and closing hours and she would tell Custódio that he had to go and get the letters in order to find out what had happened long, long ago, when there was still some hope for Walter—"Custódio, don't forget the letters." He would struggle to the post office. His lightest cart was drawn by an equally light gray mule, which struggled along the new roads under construction. He came back with another letter in his shirt pocket. He opened it at the table. It was from Luís Dias.

79.

Luís Dias, the one who, all those years ago, used to demolish houses, plank by plank, was now writing to ask if there was any truth in the rumor that had gone around Hamilton between 1964 and 1965.

He didn't even know how to begin, but basically the matter can be summarized as follows—The story being told in his city at the time was that Walter had traveled around Valmares in the Chevrolet with the blanket in the trunk, and that he had first tried to get Maria Ema to lie down on the blanket with him and then his own daughter. Now that his niece was an adult, why shouldn't Luís Dias speak freely? At first, the word in Hamilton was that the only reason it hadn't happened was because Custódio Dias had taken care of his wife and niece, watching over them day and night. Later, the word was that it really had happened. But only the three of them, Maria Ema, Custódio and Francisco Dias, as living witnesses, could say whether or not it was true. He and his wife would like to know. And the present-day builder and former demolisher of houses added at the end of his letter—"May God forgive me if all I'm doing is repeating a lie. I hate lies and liars, along with all the other vices. I always have"—*From Luís Dias, Hamilton.*

And the supposedly last letter is from the miner, the one in Ottawa, who used to wear a tin or metal helmet with a light on it so that he could see the ore and who now owns limousines and taxis. With lots of lights and headlights so as to have a clear view of those long, wide roads. He sees from a distance and interprets—His niece's rumored way of life is clearly due to some traumatic experience she had with Walter, her uncle or father, as you wish.

The fact is that Walter must have had some reason for driving around in a Chevrolet that didn't belong to him, with that soldier's blanket always at the ready. Manuel Dias may live far away, but he can see exactly what might have happened. Or what did happen. May God forgive him if, from Ottawa, he sees far too much in Valmares and São Sebastião. It's not his fault if he sees so much and with such certainty across all that distance in time and space. My God, the things he sees!—Dear Pa, dear brother, dear sister-in-law, dear niece whom I haven't seen for so long, and who, when I left her, was just a little girl and who, now, I would love to see settled, married, happy and living in prosperity and peace. "But that clearly wasn't God's plan. All the best"—*From Manuel Dias, Limo Service, Ottawa.*

There was nothing to say. In Valmares the sun was setting, persimmon red, behind the smooth fields. Custódio, Maria Ema and Francisco Dias were incapable of interpreting the complex reality that rose up from the past landscape of their lives as described in those last letters.

It was as if Francisco Dias' sons were gathered together in some extraordinary place, outside the Earth, up there where the satellites bob, and yet that place was also São Sebastião de Valmares. It was as if they had never left the original parish, the old church, or what used to be the courtyard of this house, and were revisiting those places, step by step, tree by tree, in order to pursue Walter's fantastical crime. For them, 1981 was farther off than 1962, and 1962 was farther off than 1951. But the epicenter of all the commotion was the rainy winter of 1963. They spoke of the muddy paths along which Walter would have seduced his daughter, the big houses he would have lured her into on the pretext of showing her drawings of meadow pipits and redstarts, the rolled-up blanket which he lay at her feet when he took her to hotels in Faro in the Chevrolet that didn't belong to him. The train, the station, the houses, the trees, the people they mentioned were from twenty or thirty years ago, seen from that distance through a punishing, furious, poisonous eye—As I said, a revenge for something that never happened and for an imagined victim was being served up ice-cold. Custódio no longer opened those foolish, fetid letters. He said he tore them up. And when they became telephone calls, he stopped picking up the receiver. The phone would ring for hours. For a while, no one answered the phone at all. "Let it ring, don't pick it up"–Custódio would say to Maria Ema. "No, you're right"–she would say. I am remembering this tonight so that Walter will know.

80.

Eventually, the poisoned letters stopped coming. Their authors seemed to return for good to the interior, to the snow, to the foot of a pile of planks, to the cement dust, to the railway lines, to the flat grazing lands, except that now they sat atop their new fortunes, their gold-paved roads, their invisible money swelling like a river. They vanished, disappeared, they had been part of life, but they had also been a dream. The poisoned circular letters burned themselves out, leaving a detritus of shadows that had lasted two years, and all for nothing. I do not intend to return to those letters.

If I mention them it is only because the abomination they created is part of the web woven about Walter. Walter would not be complete tonight, before his soldier's blanket, if the image of debauchery and lies that shaped him were not here in the house in Valmares. But the replies to Custódio Dias disappear, as do the phone calls. Francisco Dias' energy disappears too. Now, above the stones and olive trees, proper roads are opening up to form intersections, solid, black rivers buzzing with wheels heading off to other places. He doesn't go to see them, he neither can nor wants to, all that fast-moving traffic means nothing to him. And when Walter's daughter tells him they should have been built thirty years ago, he says–"Well, why don't you just drive off down one of them and disappear!"

"What time did she come in?"–asked Maria Ema, who had fallen asleep with her clothes on. Custódio went over to his wife, his lame foot dragging, his winged foot marking the regular beating of the world's other clock—"I'm not sure, but it wasn't that late." He was lying. Both had happened to be walking in the courtyard. When you heard the footsteps of one, you could always expect to hear the footsteps of the other as well. Sometimes, it was as if Maria Ema were walking along keeping time with Custódio Dias. Maria Ema seemed to be limping too.

The first umbrellas date from that period, the first modern deck chairs, the first climbing plants that Custódio gave to Maria Ema so that she could rebuild her life. Nothing much, just a few new objects that would require other things in the house to be changed, creating the illusion of an internal revolution. Certain eras hiding underneath other eras, matter replacing matter, for the refreshment of the soul. The weary body taking pleasure in small things. She would sit in the old courtyard. "Isn't this lovely!" she would say.

81.

But Francisco Dias would stay by the door of the house. He still wants nothing to do with deck chairs, he can't adapt. He prefers a mahogany chair with solid arms, so that he can sit up straight, looking around him, but across an ever-shortening radius. Sometimes, though, he goes up the stairs. I can hear him panting as he climbs. He would like to be odorless and silent, but he can be neither. He would like to watch unseen what she does in her room. For some time now, he has feared that she might be painting birds, which is the last thing he wants her to do with her life. It would be worse than her opening the front door at five in the afternoon and setting off in the direction of the vanished Dr. Dalila, worse than her not saying where she's going, worse than her not coming back, than her coming back and refusing to say where she's been or who with, or who she's brought back with her, worse than her not talking, or driving off in the Dyane at an hour when she should be coming back. That is why Francisco Dias goes up the stairs, opens the door, making the kind of noise he was hoping to avoid, in order to observe Walter's daughter; after all, who knows what she might be doing shut up in her room.

Yes, the king of the scrublands comes to spy. He says he no longer has control over anything or anyone, but, in that winter of 1981, he goes up to his granddaughter's room, breathing hard, to make it quite clear he is spying. He wants to know what she's doing, shut up in the house, when outside the fields are green and damp. He wants to know, he wants to go up in order to find out, he wants to open the bolted door, beating on it with one of his crutches. It occurs to him to issue some order to the daughter of his youngest son, to stop her from doing something, just what he doesn't know, but to stop her from doing something, anything. He will go up to the landing to see what she's doing and stop her from doing it. Francisco Dias' last journeys are between his room on the ground floor and the stairs going up to the room on the first floor. His granddaughter is not totally without pity, which is why she comes downstairs and talks to him. Indeed, they speak to each other on the last morning. They even argue, get angry with each other, insult each other, they're so alike.

But Francisco Dias should never have got angry with his

granddaughter, who was his opponent and his captive too. He should have realized from the start that she would never entirely leave his world, and that if he wanted to keep someone in Valmares as a remnant of all that had been lost, he could leave the world with an easy mind, because she would stay. Or, rather, she does stay. Unlike the others who went and never came back, she goes, but she always comes back. She is bound to Custódio's lame foot, to his wife, to his trees, to the vanished chickens, to the last eggs, to the last farm gate, to the last collars and halters, she is bound to the last farm implements. She cannot help herself. All the letters she writes will be about those dead objects lying on the ground, hanging from the walls, outside in the rain, in the moonlit puddles in the barns, the contraptions on the winding bar on the wells, the buckets on the water wheel, she is bound to the deaths of the servants and to the young girls who drowned, to the ferns that grow in green clumps and disguise the green backs of the toads. She is bound to the toad, to the dark salamander with the crooked tail, to the poplar, to the cypress, to the white cemetery where her ancestors' bones lie crumbling, their names bound to the earth, until they vanish into the abyss of forgetting, where perhaps Dr. Dalila's gravestone also lies. She is bound to the hidden hearts of the stones. She never leaves, she simply returns. Before, she used to go with one man and come back with another, to whom she would say goodbye after exchanging long kisses at the door, she would come back with another who kissed differently, then she would fall out with men, not knowing how to deal with them or not wanting to keep them. In 1980, Maria Ema, standing at the window, used to say her daughter would end up alone, that she didn't know how to hold on to a man, and that she had no luck because God wasn't on her side. She shouted the same thing right to her face, she said she didn't want any more scandals, any more men, she didn't want to see any more faces or to get their names wrong, though just in case she did, she never even asked who they were anymore. At the time, she was still worried about what the neighbors would think. Except that there weren't any neighbors. As I said, Maria Ema's main neighbors were the genet and the fox. But Custódio's wife didn't realize that. Then she found out. She was alone, beneath the umbrellas, sitting on a deck chair, waiting for her husband. On at least one occasion, she called to him—"Are you there, love?" Just so that Walter will know on this night when we meet over his soldier's blanket.

82.

Because after the letters, a greater understanding developed between the two of them, a symmetrical behavior as if one were the echo of the other. Custódio would say to Maria Ema—"So the Chevrolet wasn't his, then." And following him along the path to the courtyard gate that both of them pushed shut, she would reply—"No, apparently it wasn't." Despite having no new facts, they were sure now. And when they came back, they would look at Walter's daughter, as if to say—No, that car wasn't his.

Then the daughter would think that the arrival by taxi wasn't his either, nor the rain that had brought them together, nor the drives along the N125. The wanderings through the house weren't his, nor was the warm embrace he gave her on the morning when he lit the bonfire before day dawned, nor his departure sliding over the glassy ice, which she would hear for a decade afterward. The subsequent silence that accompanied that decade wasn't his, nor the irony she had grown accustomed to like an invisible shield. The fifteen-year silence that she herself had built to keep out the people of that house was not his. The Smith revolver, the metal bullets, his life, none of those things were his. And although there was no explaining where that analogy began and ended, and even if almost all the poison letters could be shown to be nothing but fantasy, everything was a lie because the Chevrolet was not his. Some remnant of her old pride must have been working away inside Walter's daughter's head, a pride made up of sacred duties to do with money, an archaic scruple, an archaeological honor lost in the newly changed world and which still existed engraved on her mind, because that was the only way she could accept that the Chevrolet continued to drive in her direction, but that it no longer carried the same passengers—Walter Dias and Maria Ema Baptista—as it had in the winter of 1963. Gradually the Chevrolet was becoming no more than a luxurious black tin can that occasionally swept noiselessly past, headed who knows where.

83.

But in the whole life of a person, how can the image of a car running on velvet wheels compare with the rainy night when he visited his daughter? So, before we say goodbye, we must call up more memories tonight so that Walter will know.

In Valmares, letters continued to be placed on the same bureau in the corridor, on the back wall, between two doors and two vases, where the bird album first took shape. That was where Custódio had piled up his brothers' letters, and that was where she went to read them, sometimes involuntarily learning them by heart. After some months had passed, that was where she found some new handwritten sheets, slipped into what she had thought were the last letters from the Dias brothers. They belonged to the letters Custódio had refused to read or had not given to anyone else to read, or had not even mentioned receiving. There were about five, possibly six, and among them was one from Manuel Dias, the one who used to be a miner with a lamp on his head, a bucket with iron ore on his arm, beads of sweat on his face, and who now owned a fleet of cars and had a transatlantic vision of what had happened in Valmares in 1963. In one part of the letter, he said—"You wouldn't want to hide anything from me, would you, Custódio? When he came here to show us photographs of your children, he himself told me that he used to go into his daughter's room, in his stocking feet, his shoes in his hand, while you were all sleeping. May I be struck deaf and dumb and be condemned to a miserable old age in the worst insane asylum in Ontario if that is not what he told me. Why would Walter invent something like that? And now you say it didn't happen. Perhaps you were too angry, but you must have been stone blind not to have seen anything..." And then Manuel Dias closed by saying that he might manage to free himself from engagements the following year in order, finally, to come and sort out the matter of Valmares—*From Manuel Dias, Limo Service, Ottawa.*

That meant that he himself had told them.

Sometimes, standing by the bureau fitted into that wall as thick as a city wall, she thought it simply wasn't possible, that some vital words spoken by Walter must have been left out, that Walter, in leisurely conversation with his brother, must have said something very different, something logical and true. She imagined he might have said—Do you know, in order for us to have a few words alone, I had to go up to the room where she was sleeping, and in order not to alarm anyone, I waited for a rainy night and I even took off my shoes. I loved her and all of them and I didn't want to hurt any of them. I never wanted to hurt anyone... She imagined he would have said that to Manuel Dias, but the brother in Ottawa, thinking only of the money Walter owed him, would have heard different words, or the same ones, but with different intonations and accompanying noises. And so she forgave Walter, and Walter again came up the stairs to her room whenever she wanted him to. Only it wasn't like before, he didn't glow in the darkness, he was neither happy nor sad, he was just a gesturing shadow and then not even that, more like someone dead. He was gradually fading away.

84.

Yes, the almond trees were covered with petals at the end of that winter, in warm, damp February. It was as if those intricate trees did not even exist among the other trees until their fragile branches suddenly sprouted petals. A veil of petals emerged from that network of nothing, covering the fields, joining them together, as if a white wind had blown over the land in order to prove the earth was still alive. That fine, gentle flowering happened then and only then. The rarely trodden paths were covered by carpets of petals that survived for days without disintegrating, and when they did, Walter's daughter thought of reinvigorated nature challenging that unrepeatable transience.

She thought of the way natural images reveal the irreversible passing of life. She thought of red poppies waving on the surface of the wheat fields after battles, as if the blood of men had been transformed into the flowers of their homeland, and other similar scenes that fill the tragic pages of a country's history and are later set to music after the armistices are signed. At the end of that winter, as she walked those paths, she could not help thinking about the snowy battle in the hills of the Ardennes, contemporary with Walter. She went back in time and thought of the French soldiers returning from icebound Moscow, she invoked random images of other battles, and then thought of Hector, whom she had suffered with during the years of *The Iliad*, Hector dead and borne in pomp upon a carriage before the walls of Troy. How could she invoke other disparate images, limited as she was by the insignificance of the vague facts at her disposal, all mixed up with other private memories stored in the soul, when confronted by the great absolute that was always happening and that never repeated itself and never stopped—that great flowing sea? But above the infinitely insignificant things of which her memory retained only fragments, and above that vast, infinite, external sea slipping swiftly by, there arose, vigorous and real, what she herself loved. She had known for a long time that on certain rainy nights, the history of humankind was less important to her than the history of her father, however wrong it seemed to think such a thing, let alone say it or even whisper it. And that is why she wished that Walter, whom people had nicknamed soldier Walter, had died on a battlefield.

There was no need for him to have been a hero, or for his name to have been mentioned on the radio or even inscribed on a wall, she merely wished he had disappeared, wrapped in a blanket, in a piece of gray serge, and had never given rise to those letters. She envied the dead whose bodies had never returned home and of whom no one knew anything, of whom nothing remained, not even the prong of a buckle. With the cruelty of her thirty years, she wished Walter definitively dead so that he could never have come back to fill the glorious days of 1963, to disturb lame Custódio's peace, to set Maria Ema's otherwise steady path ablaze. She would have preferred him to be a figure buried in the outer vastness that had nothing to do with her. That's what she would have preferred. She thought about it for hours on end. And walking over the thin layer of white and pink petals from the almond blossoms, which stuck to the soles of her feet and which she brought into the house like a second sole, not bothering to wipe them on the wire mat by the door, she realized that she could not go on living unless she destroyed Walter's life.

85.

She began this insidious work, which consisted in destroying Walter's very person, by creeping slowly into her own small room, like a spy. She didn't want anyone, no matter who, telling her to leave her room, or bothering her about when to sleep or eat. She wanted to journey into the interior of Walter. She wanted to attack him silently from inside, to pierce, transfix, reduce, destroy his person, corrupting him, transforming his sweet, evanescent immateriality into a parabola of carnality in order to make him disappear. She was going into that territory so as to snuff out, to murder the person she loved, in the very place she had always judged to be invulnerable. To murder him with a sleeping potion, a cup of mandrake. In her stocking feet, with her shoes in her hand, just as he had taught her, she was intent on profanation. She would profane his bones like a microbe, delving into the internal network of bones and into the soft pulp of the heart. This was her abominable task. In the spring of 1983, the soldier's blanket superimposed itself on everything else like a reason to hate. In the silence of her room, this same room, while the trees lost their blossoms, the stems wrapped themselves in green leaves, and the sap-filled branches multiplied and offered up small bunches of fruits enclosed in suede skins, the necessary words, natural and cold, came to her effortlessly, painlessly. It was toward the end of that warm winter that she began to write about Walter. She knew, as the Dias brothers had always known, that in order to do real harm to someone's reputation, you have to start with their sex life. She had to start with Walter's sex life.

Where were the letters and the drawings of birds? They had been put away, but they would be taken out, opened, methodically leafed through, becoming mere objects of interest, collectibles, in the library of her coldness. Once more I summon up the coldness surrounding the interesting case study Walter Dias had now become. Defiance, the vengeful side of scorn, filled her days during that flowering, silent spring. The vigorous branches gave her sufficient presence of mind to write unpleasant sentences of cold defense, like a paid lawyer, as analytical as a physician before a body. Through the window that opened onto the grass, she viewed Walter like a clinical case, she spoke of him, when necessary, as a product, explained him away by his childhood experiences, the way cold people do, casting over the fate of others the web of the explanatory spider, the rough web of cause irreversibly generating effect. She did this to Walter. She wanted in this way to capture him, extinguish him, get beyond him, forget him and be free. She wrote three stories aimed at Walter. I remember those cold stories, those icy tales, written against a man who had fed the lives of people with dog-eared drawings of birds. Then Maria Ema, surprised to see her daughter spending so much time at home, leaving her old Dyane parked in the yard, would call up to her—"Are you still there?" Yes, and she would be for a few more months. When the stories were written, she would set out to find Walter. It wouldn't be hard.

86.

It was fairly likely that Walter would have continued on down the South American continent. He couldn't have gone far— Walter was beginning to be hemmed in by the vastness of the world. She imagined that he would avoid Africa, where he did not wish to return, so he would be unlikely to leave the western Atlantic coast. Just as he had predicted, Africa was in flames, each scrap of land bitterly disputed, and the new tyrants seemed as barbarous as the old ones, with the added disadvantage that they were the blood relatives of those they tyrannized. He had been right. The green palm trees were still the same, but their arms swayed in a different wind, a wind filled with bullets. The transatlantic steamers no longer crossed the seaways, with orchestras on board to ease those adventurous journeys. The big ships were grounded, rusting in ports, cannibalized for spare parts or visited as relics. Iron dinosaurs, displaying their jaws near empty docks. Pursued by change, Walter would, thought his daughter, have traveled on down the coast of South America. He must have headed in the direction of Brazil or Buenos Aires. It was almost predictable. She knew. She could sense it in its essence and substance, though she lacked actual circumstantial evidence. That took a while to obtain, but was eventually provided by the Argentinian Embassy. Since 1981, Walter Dias had resided on Calle Marina. And when they told her he owned a bar on Calle Morgana, the daughter could not resist asking sarcastically if its name, by any chance, had anything to do with birds. The person on the other end said—"Yes, it does, actually, it's called Los Pájaros—The Birds."

It was autumn again. Maria Ema stood at the door to watch the Dyane leaving—"Won't you even tell us where you're going? You never tell us anything."

Los Pájaros. I went in search of Los Pájaros.

The distant soldier of 1945 is now a man who lives in Argentina. She has to go in search of that person, that attractive cyclops, it really doesn't matter what names you call him, so bruised are we all by the passing of time. In her bag she was carrying three fantastic tales, attacks on the seductive figure, both present and absent, who had given them life.

Besides, it seemed ironic that Walter should end up where he did. At the time, people still spoke of Argentina as a clandestine slaughterhouse. It was said that law-abiding citizens continued to be taken from their houses by armed silhouettes, faceless shadows, who bundled their captives into fast cars that bore them away never to be seen again. There were extraordinary rumors about prisoners being thrown out of airplanes, far from the coast, to the south, toward Tierra del Fuego, or else to the north, near Punta del Este, and some of them over the Caribbean. So people said. Between the airport and Buenos Aires, in that month of October, the yellow plain still smelled of butcher's shops and gunpowder. On certain days, the Plaza de Mayo was still full of women wearing white headscarves, demanding the return of the disappeared. The fact was that their children had been obliterated, but the government hired people to say they were in good health and would be returned as soon as they cooperated with the police. A tangle of living ghosts, the magical cortège of all tyrannies. It was in the middle of this disguised butcher's shop that I found Walter Dias, the owner of Los Pájaros.

87.

I summon up Los Pájaros and its door on Calle Morgana, number 43, its high, turn-of-the-century windows, its fine wood paneling, its yellow wall and the words inscribed on a metal sign—BAR LOS PÁJAROS. No one goes in and no one comes out. The bar is still closed, as ill-lit night falls on Buenos Aires. She realizes that there is no distance at all between the door of that house and the track down which Walter disappeared for the last time, heading for the Valmares road, with the headlights off. At that moment, he is just the same. She still expects the black Chevrolet to appear at the bottom of the road, to drive up, stop and park on the pavement, and to see a man in a light raincoat and dark suit step out and walk toward the door. What will she say? What should she call him? Uncle Walter? She can see him coming into her room, seizing the oil lamp and holding it up to her face, as always. It's not possible, everything they wrote was a lie, a powerful family fiction with which the Dias brothers fill imaginations that have become disconnected from their homeland, their cozy fantasy, like dead fish rotting on the shore, thinks the daughter as, for hours, she walks up and down, waiting for the black Chevrolet to arrive.

Nevertheless, she knows that, according to Luísa Dias, Walter had bought first a Chrysler, then a Studebaker, then a white Mustang. After that, she doesn't know. There is no Chevrolet now. All that exists is a twenty-year gap, no, not twenty, one hundred, five thousand, eight thousand if you consider *The Iliad*. The distance between identity and dispersal cannot be measured in years or even centuries. She spends hours outside the bar that only opens at 11:00. Walking up and down, she doesn't know what she is doing so far from Valmares, since she hasn't anything to give Walter, apart from an archaic tale in three chapters which she wants to tell to the man himself. She doesn't know why she has come to trouble him, nor why she must to do this, why she can't survive without this meeting. She has inside her shoulder bag not a loaded revolver, but three tales to hand over. What good would a real revolver do there? Occasionally people go in and come out. Walter neither goes in nor comes out. She goes in. I remember that entrance, I apologize for it, not for going in, but for the cold way in which she crossed the threshold of that house with just a touch of the brothel about it. But she goes in.

88.

She goes in, and no one's there. She looks around at the interior of Los Pájaros. It's a solid wood-paneled design from the 1940s. In fact, everything looks old, frozen in time, contemporary with the Peróns and their mixture of charity and extravagance. She goes in. The wood paneling, the high tables, the heavy chairs which seem to be made out of whole branches of exotic trees, even the leather upholstery seems to belong to a different age. There are real buffaloes stretched over the chairs in Los Pájaros.

Los Pájaros recalls the old cafés of Faro, the buttery wax polish that smelled of must and turpentine. And smoke, it smells of cigarettes, old cigarette ash and smoke. But between the piano and the bar, something is moving. It has its back turned, fixing a piano stool, it seems to be screwing in one leg of the stool, struggling to get the leg in and you can hear the physical effort involved. There's a hammer on the floor. With some difficulty the creature bends down to pick up the hammer and calls for someone who does not come. The human shape in a checkered suit puts down the stool, stands up and turns around. Inside the broad, pale checkered shape, with a hammer in its hand, is what remains of a seducer, what remains of soldier Walter.

There is also what remains of the quartermaster, the drawer of birds, of Walter. And there is the coldness with which she addresses the bulky remains of the former sailor and merchant, Walter. Tense, despotic, protected by a complete absence of pity, the daughter sits down on a chair in front of Walter Dias.

At first, Walter doesn't look at her. Only after some time has passed and he has had a good stiff drink does he laugh. His laugh is the same. The room fills when he recovers his laugh. His face has grown fat, but in the middle of that face his old features remain intact. His limbs have bulked out, his trunk has taken on a bullish corpulence, but the broad shape of his limbs, beneath that surface of gray, white and black checks, is the same. His shirt collar is pale, pointed, sharp. His slender patent-leather shoes have pointed toes that click across the floor like women's shoes. He is dressed as people used to dress in the past, although it is very hard to pinpoint that past, which is farther back than the time of his visit to Valmares, that glorious day that lasted almost three months. She looks at the objects in the bar. She has always known that objects are a very intimate part of someone's being. There he was, surrounded by his objects. There he was, overwhelmed by the presence of his former niece, the thief on the stairs, the one who had made him go up to her room on that rainy night against his will, perhaps against his wishes. Crestfallen and ashamed before his daughter— "Would you like something to drink?"

"*¿Qué quieres?* What would you like? What do you want to drink?"—Nothing, she doesn't want anything.

89.

Then the bar fills with European music, with music of every homesick hue. Neapolitan music, Andalusian, French, Polish music, Romanian music. A selection he himself made using his antiquated record player, recorded onto an ancient tape. In the intervals between the music, you can hear the hiss of the tape. It's a well-cared-for old machine. The music comes out fuzzy. It is interlaced with Argentinian music. Sad *milongas,* rodeo music, the melancholy music of the pampas. Tango music. Astor Piazzolla. The people there, drinking and smiling, are stiff and proud, they seem to have just arrived from some endless plain, similar to the sea. I think they come from the sea and the flat land, with no other horizon than the horizon itself, that line which is always moving farther off. And Walter knows, he hasn't lost his touch, because the people who come into the bar address him familiarly, as if they were friends, it's clear he is someone of importance in that circle. Around one o'clock in the morning, Walter's bar is full. He says it's only then that things start to happen. He sits down at the table where he told her to sit and complains about the night, about fear, about the police, the military, the bankers, his suppliers, he complains about everything to do with Calle Morgana. He complains about the local diet and puts the blame for his extra weight on that, saying he dreams of going back to a different life. It's a country of too much meat. He says families even feed babies on the juices from the cooked meat. And then there was the maté tea. He hated maté. The mystique of meat seemed to him somehow profane and troubling. Meat troubled him— *"Me perturba muchísimo..."* The fact that he kept using Spanish and drawled, hybrid words seemed indecent, strange. It was as if he had bowed to something that dragged him down, not because it was Spanish, but because it wasn't him, the person he used to be. It was that *"Me perturba muchísimo,"* uttered in the same singsong tones that she could hear all around her, which gave her the energy to spread out on the wooden table the papers she had in her bag.

But first, she asks about his drawings of birds. The daughter's coldness is primed and ready. None of her questions is innocent. They are not studied questions, but they are arrows nevertheless, and he, unaware of that, tells the truth—"I've done skimmers, swallows, plovers, parrots, black-headed gulls, oh, loads and loads of them. But I'm a bit tired of drawing. Why replicate them with my hand when they're all in here, in my head?" Yes, of course, he still draws, but very little now. She asks him for the fifth time why he doesn't draw anymore. He says for the tenth time that he doesn't need to. He did put some drawings up in the tango salon, around the dance floor. But they didn't look right, they seemed out of keeping with the couples dancing. Now he prefers to have nothing on the walls— "Don't you like the place?" Everything is happening so quickly. He doesn't even ask her why she's interrogating him, he's on the defensive, strangely surprised, he's intelligent, he knows she hasn't come to give him anything, but, rather, to take something from him, he knows this is a settling of accounts. And so he says—"Why imitate nature? Nature exists for its own sake, without me. I still think about birds, but they're out there on the pampas without me copying them. I don't need to draw any more birds, they're all inside my head, but you only know that when you get older. No, I don't need to draw them in order to see them. Birds…"

90.

The conversation becomes strained, he knows why she has come, but he doesn't know how she is going to carry out her intention, and she doesn't want to act just yet, she's afraid that if she shows him what she has brought, he might stop the conversation and order everyone out of the bar. He doesn't ask about her or about Maria Ema or even about Custódio, nor about

Portugal and its new government, nor about Valmares. Walter is imprisoned by the surprise that has befallen him. He used to have three cars and two houses, he says. But here a man can wake up owning several cars and several houses and go to sleep owning nothing. Mixing up the two languages, he says *coches* not *carros*. Owning large houses and cars was the only way to keep your money alive. He didn't ask about Maria Ema or about Custódio, or about the house in Valmares, nor even why his daughter was there, nor how she had located him, nor how she had got there, nor why she was looking for him. It was as if surprise, or the expectation of what was coming, had annihilated him or left him willing to be led. There was no point in doing anything about that annihilation. When she held out to him the bundles of papers that contained the abominable tales she had come to give him, he took them. "Gracias"—he said.

Besides, beneath the weight of that visit to his nest, the nest of an old bird, he would happily have accepted a shot from a revolver. If she had still owned it and had taken it out and shot him, he would have found that perfectly natural. Deep down, he had been expecting this surprise for ages. And then, when those slow, proud people, with their 1940s-style brilliantined hair, with a mixture of Italian and Indian in their olive skin, with a hint too of Galician and French parentage, when those dark-skinned people, with dark, profoundly sad souls composed of a complete inability to be supremely happy, something she knew so well from her own country, when they started to leave, laughing that long, sad, elegant laugh, slurring their words, pronouncing them with the fewest possible movements of the tongue, with voices that emerged from the back of the mouth, half kiss, half yawn, the men pressing the women to their belt buckles as if they were guitars, and the women surrendering to them as if they were their instruments, when that happened and we were left almost alone, with just two couples performing brusque movements in the half dark, like dancers in dreams, I held out to Walter Dias the first bundle of papers.

He took out his glasses, using the same gestures as when he put on his sunglasses to drive the Chevrolet in 1963, the same gestures as when he had touched Maria Ema's arms, in front of us all, on the way back from Sagres, and he began to read. He only stopped to ask his daughter if it was all her own work. "¡Preciosísimo!"–he said, reading slowly, the reading of someone with only partial sight, of someone deciphering each word in a very dim light. And then he read obediently, sipping, smiling, in his checkered suit, hidden beneath that mound of flesh that did not belong to him, but came from the barbecue grills, from the fat of plump steers, cut up and smoked over those grills. And while he did so, and even though she had given him that chalice to drink from, his daughter loved him. She loved him, not the man he could have been, but the man sitting there reading those abominable pages, straining at the words like a blind man, smiling awkwardly at his daughter, bent over the pages which he kept untidily shuffling. Walter read.

91.

He read out loud, he read slowly, he read softly, he read in Spanish and in Portuguese as if he were reading in another language, seated vastly in the middle of that brown, mirrored bar built on different levels, with a silent piano and an area where the four tango dancers occasionally wrapped about each other. The women surrendered to the men, vanquished, compliant, relenting. He was facing the tango floor as he was reading. Every now and then he would say—"¡Che!" As detached from what he was reading as he was from himself. He was reading the story innocently, not realizing it was about himself. He was reading in the Argentine night, which was neither hot nor cold, but stretched out silently along the length of an immense port. He was reading. *"Muy bien, muy bien"*—he said. "Did you write all this?" His daughter said she had. And she was touched by a sense of sadness for that slow, heavy man, his curly hair sticking to his temples, so far from Lake Ontario where he would have liked to have stayed, at least for a little while longer. That man who no longer made drawings of birds touched her heart. And Walter's daughter was once more visited by vulnerability, because he did not understand the parable she was offering him, the coarse, offensive, barbarous metaphor she had delivered to him, firsthand. He probably hadn't even read the title. He hadn't seen it.

Walter Dias could not understand the sheaf of papers he was holding in his hand, under the rather dim lamp he had placed on the table. The story he was reading, while the last pair of tango dancers swayed and executed swift turns, after several moments during which they had seemed fixed in a jar in formaldehyde, only to awaken in each other's arms, shake themselves, then stop again, bodies closely entwined, as I said, the story he was reading and which he read without really reading it, was about a fierce, sarcastic and, at the same time, trivial ghost, as if described by Dr. Dalila. An invention with just a touch of Carnival and whisky about it. The story of a very old, very wealthy, very smug man, who suddenly had the idea of gathering together all his children in order to share out his fortune among them and teach them the art of living well and of succeeding.

How can I put it?

The man in the story had not always been rich. When very young, he had been a poor soldier traveling from port to port getting involved in shady deals and engendering children on various beaches along the coasts of the Portuguese Empire, all achievements he was very proud of. And now, in order to prove to his children that he was their progenitor, he had taken the precaution of coming properly equipped, for he had kept the earth-stained blanket on which he had lain with women of various colors and languages. According to him, the things that had happened on that blanket had made it unforgettable. When he arrived at a port, all he had to do was whistle in a certain way, and all the women who had ever slept with him would come running, assuming they were still alive or in a reasonable state of health. His interests were now quite different, of course. The very wealthy old man was to make the journey on a steamship, accompanied by two servants and an explorer, who would help him to find his legitimate descendants scattered among the coastal towns, through the mark left by his own features, those unmistakable family traits. And so they had set off. Except that, when they did arrive at ports and bays, it was difficult to recognize the descendants left behind by the former soldier, because they had interbred with other mammals, and now when he returned to his old haunts, he found his eyes imprinted on both people and animals, who all followed him, drawn by the smell of the earth-stained blanket. How it ended didn't matter. Helped aboard his steamship by his two servants and the explorer, the very wealthy, very old soldier, his Panama hat on his head, was followed by a nonhuman tribe with whom he could neither talk nor share out the spoils. Laden with people and animals, all with the same pale eyes, the steamship continued its voyage across the sea. If Walter had read on, he would have known that they never encountered an island. The story Walter held in his hands was merely an expansion of Adelina Dias' image of the atlas. She herself, the daughter, was one of the Dias family. It was a coarse, abominable parable in crude language, with an obvious title. The only reason he didn't understand was that he wasn't really reading it.

92.

He wasn't reading it because he was still in a state of shock, for although he might have imagined being surprised, the surprise took forms he had not foreseen, trapped as he was in the heart of his refuge. Only when his daughter held out to him both "The Painter of Birds" and "The Devil's Chariot" did he go back and read the title of the fierce little tale he had glanced over but not read, and only then did he sense that his daughter was offering him not sheaves of paper, but a mirror. He blushed. He began to leaf back and forth through the three bundles of paper. He almost dropped them. He looked at his daughter, who looked back at him and at the papers beneath the dim light. Walter Dias read the title of the first story out loud—"'The Fornicating Soldier.' 'Fornicating...,'" he said again. And then, terrified—"You didn't write this, did you?" The murmurous night still clung to that wood-lined room. Soldier Walter, deathly pale, lifted up his great body, a body too heavy for his skeleton, a body that hung from his skeleton as if dragging with it the material nature of the places it had passed through and from which it had been unable to free itself, and, in the middle of the music-filled, dance-filled room, he brandished the papers, trembling with rage. "Get out, get out of here!"—he said. The couple who were still swaying, half-asleep, on the dance floor woke up. "Get out!"

Walter Dias could not allow such a fantasy to be written about his blanket. His blanket was the place on which he had drawn his birds and done whatever else he wanted to do. It was none of anyone else's business. His hatred for his daughter's words was growing. Standing up, he read whole passages out loud, in Portuguese with an Algarve accent and with not a word of Spanish, as if his rage had transported him back to his origins. His hatred was an old one, similar to the hatred his daughter had seen in certain men in Valmares. It was a barbarous hatred that sent tables and chairs flying, that flung out at her the names of different members of the family, each one accompanied by an insult. I was the family in question. In response to these shouts, the woman of the last tango couple put a mantilla over her head, in the old-fashioned style, and left, gripping the elbow of her tango partner. "Get out!"

It was growing light on Calle Morgana, it was growing light as it had twenty years before in Valmares, but everything was happening in reverse. Instead of the embrace he had given her then, he was driving his daughter and her verminous papers away, because of that sordid, barbarous act of revenge. "Get out!" It was no longer night. I summon the anger of soldier Walter into this night tonight. He went and stood breathless and angry at the door on Calle Morgana, outside Los Pájaros, one finger raised. I see that anger, I postpone it, delay it, multiply it. The anger of that night will always remain part of my own anger, it will be an integral part of my most private legacy. Later on.

93.

The truth is that his daughter had not gone to Los Pájaros to bring him consolation, but for her own benefit. She had gone there in order to cut something that needed to be cut, when it needed to be cut. To cut into herself. That is why she took those steps.

She will spend the following night strolling up and down that straight, new road, which to Argentinians seemed old, she will keep watch on him from Calle Marina and will try to speak to him. She remembers. She has her back turned, in the middle of Calle Morgana, waiting for him. He passes her, crosses her path, and both feign complete indifference, as if their paths had not in fact crossed, he goes in and she stays out in the street, by the sign saying BAR LOS PÁJAROS. It is a clear October in Buenos Aires, the weather is as mild at night as it is during the day or at sunset. She stands outside, determined to wait. Until he comes out, in those thin-soled shoes in which his feet and the steps he takes seem superfluous. The patent leather toe caps bear a punched-out design, like the shoes Fred Astaire used to wear. He walks ponderously over to her. Walter asks after Maria Ema and Custódio Dias, he asks what happened to Francisco Dias. It's better to go like that, without realizing, he says, much better. And he made as if to disappear back inside that house of dark wood out of which seeped the sounds of music and dancing, but the daughter had come there for another reason—"What do you want, then?"

It was simple, she didn't want anything from him, just to know why he drew birds, but he was already heading back into Los Pájaros. "Wait!"—she said, before he did so. He owed her that. But he pretended not to understand and was saying goodbye—"I don't know." He didn't have any particular reason, he just drew them, he always had, he said, heading for the door and stopping her from going in.—Wait, you owe me a reply! Did Walter really think he could go through life unpunished? That it was just a matter of getting bored and leaving? She wanted to know. And his daughter went over to him and asked him once and for all why he drew all those birds, begging him not to lie to her. He had spent his whole life drawing, he had wasted his time and his reputation drawing birds in whichever place he happened to be passing through, and now he was telling her it had all been for nothing? Didn't he see how important it was for her to have an answer? And he, clearly wanting simply to vanish from her sight, to disappear as soon as possible through that door, said—"Don't kid yourself, I did it because it gave me pleasure, that's all."

How was that possible? He had drawn the birds with such precision, copied them with the accuracy of an ornithologist, sent them back from lands through which he had traveled like a zoologist, an illustrator, a geographer of birds, sometimes like an artist. His birds often seemed ready to leap off the page, to move, to fly. His birds almost danced. Wait. She pleaded. But she stopped when she realized she was torturing him. It wasn't worth it. He said—"I don't want you to learn anything from me. I have nothing to teach you…" Wait. "I'll write to you"—he said. And he said something else too, some word of farewell, but then he went slowly in and pushed the door to, closing it in her face. The door of Bar Los Pájaros, Calle Morgana, Buenos Aires. Extraordinarily slowly. And he said—"Give my regards to her, to Maria Ema."

This, then, is so that Walter will know.

94.

In Valmares, Maria Ema liked to sit on the deck chairs in the shade of the blue umbrellas and watch the serrated line of hotels growing day by day in the distance, amidst the clearings of trees, the loud sea like a glittering belt between the line of land and sky. That was how she liked the sea to look, in fact, that was the only way she liked it, it brought her peace, she wanted the spring sea never to change, and she surrendered to the warmth of the sun spreading over the ipecacuanha. Sometimes Custódio's children would come along with a camera and take photographs of her which they got blown up and in which she was incapable of recognizing herself, she looked so different— "For heaven's sake, that's not me!" "Yes, it is!"—Custódio would say. And when her youngest son filmed her and she appeared on the screen with white hair and carrying an armful of yellow flowers, she pretended she couldn't believe what she was seeing and asked—"Isn't that Catarina Eburne?" Custódio would play along with his wife and say—"No, no, it's you on that day when you picked all the marigolds in the garden." Sometimes, too, the daughter would stop the Dyane when she passed them on the road and give them and their plants a ride. They would go for long walks, one behind the other, slow, limping journeys, in search of cuttings of good bougainvilleas. With their straw hats on their heads, they adorned the unworked fields, and people passing in cars would stop and photograph them. Sometimes the two of them would walk in the direction of the sea and look at the house that had once belonged to Dr. Dalila. "Who lives there now?"—she would ask. She didn't need Walter's regards. And I never gave them to her.

And then, years later, Adelina Dias phoned at about four o'clock in the morning during the first days of a cold November.

The phone rang out stridently, the sound leaving the low table in the hall, piercing the walls and bouncing off them, like an insinuating warning. Maria Ema and Custódio both hurried down the corridor, fearing accidents involving their sons, something to do with ambulance sirens and police messages—"Who can it be at this hour?" But it wasn't a local call, it was long-distance, from Vancouver, although it didn't sound like that when you listened, but as if Francisco Dias' daughter, who was on the other side of the world, on the Pacific Coast, were speaking from the neighboring beach. "Hello, hello? Who is it?"—said Maria Ema. "What time is it in Valmares?"—asked Adelina. The sound was so clear you could hear Fernandes— the one who had taught Walter's daughter how to make the W of Walter—talking beside his wife, but Adelina got no reply to her question. "What's wrong?"—asked Maria Ema. And the voice at the other end, which began to grow tearful, blurted out—"I'm sorry to have to say that Walter didn't leave a car, a house, a shop, a boat, a watch, a check, not even a single lousy dollar! He left absolutely nothing..." Said Adelina Dias vehemently. Maria Ema remained silent. "It's an awful thing to say about a member of the Dias family, but all he leaves behind him is a stain..." And Maria Ema still, at first, remained silent, then—"Well, what else did anyone expect, Adelina?" On the other end, Fernandes could be heard saying—"Tell them we got the news from Inácio in Caracas and that he got it from a friend of his in Argentina. Tell them." On this end, Maria Ema was explaining to Custódio—"They're saying he didn't leave a check, a suit, a single dollar, not even a house, just as we thought…" And when Maria Ema turned back to the phone, Adelina Dias had hung up.

It was better that way, because what else could be said that would justify further American expenditure? Custódio set off down the corridor, his shorter leg with its ever more certain, regular beat, sounding younger than Maria Ema's steps as they walked along. She turned to him and said—"Right, now we can rest." That is what the wife said to her husband before they went into their bedroom, just by the living room. And standing very close together, possibly with their arms about each other, they went in.

95.

"Wait"—his daughter had said before Walter went back into Bar Los Pájaros and left her in charge of all those memories. His body seemed to have an uncertain center of gravity that made him keep looking down at the ground to prevent himself from falling. Didn't he want to deny anything, contradict anything? Had he nothing to add? Didn't he want to apologize for having told Manuel Dias about what had happened on the night of rain? For never having paid back part of the cost of the Chevrolet? Or perhaps he did pay it back, but then why didn't he have the guts to say so? Didn't he want to know about the letters from his siblings so that he could deny everything they said?—"Wait." She wanted to talk about her own life, about her life with Dr. Dalila, about Dr. Dalila's successors, about the excursions in the car, about what she had done with his desk, about her plans, because she had plans, including ones that consisted purely of distancing herself from him, from her affection for him. Oh, yes, she had come in order to offend him, to get rid of the image of him that was dragging her down, and yet did he still have nothing to say? Didn't he even want to strike back at the malevolently vengeful tales she had brought for him? She was waiting. If he would only talk to her.

But he had shut the door in her face, and just before he closed it had said—"Give my regards to her, to Maria Ema." Exhausted, he was closing the door of Bar Los Pájaros, asking in Spanish, out of politeness—"*¿No querés tomar algo?* Can I get you anything? A drink perhaps..."

96.

Yes, she had come back home at peace with herself, but she had left Walter troubled forever. And she knew it. He started writing long, regular letters to Custódio, announcing his imminent return. Saying he had to come back. Hastily written letters, with no birds drawn on them. He said he wanted to come back with enough money to buy out his brothers and then give the land to Custódio, for him to do with as he wished. Unfortunately, the exchange rate was unfavorable at the moment. As a matter of fact, he had a plan, he wanted to get rich again, this time by going back up north, traveling through Mexico, California, La Paz, San Diego, San Francisco, and then on to any place where the dollar was flourishing. Perhaps head back to Ontario. In short, he wanted to return to the well-governed nations of the north. But it was clear that this was one last, final dream.

Easy money was gained by different means now. Yet in all the letters he wrote, he kept saying that, wherever he ended up, he would definitely come back. Until, finally, he too realized he would never come back. One of the letters no longer bears the name Los Pájaros. On the night that he sells Los Pájaros, he buys three cars and deposits two bags full of Argentinian peso notes in the bank. Millions of pesos, with so many zeros he got it wrong when he wrote it down. But within a matter of hours, the peso no longer exists, it has no value. By the next night, Walter's fortune is down to three cars. As we will learn later, the three cars are soon two. One day, he works out that by selling one of the cars he could buy an air ticket to New York and then a bus ticket to Newark. But, if he did that, he would arrive in Newark with no car and no money. He would have nothing. He will be reduced to one car in the Argentine nights and the vast pampas where he will find his final stopping place in his life of permanent flight. He will only stop running when he reaches the Andes, with his back to the Atlantic. And then, one cold November, there was that phone call from Adelina Dias and her husband Fernandes in Vancouver. And Maria Ema's voice, her unmistakable voice which always made me think of rosebushes, saying, "Right, now we can rest."

Wait—his daughter said. For heaven's sake, don't you understand it's important to talk about how pointless it was drawing all those birds? Don't you see? But, as I said, he just mumbled a few words in Spanish and shut the door of Bar Los Pájaros.

97.

And this morning, one of Maria Ema's sons parked his jeep on the pavement and passed the provisions he'd bought in through the window. He was in a hurry. He also tossed in a parcel from somewhere called Corrientes de Arena. A grubby parcel covered with writing. Maria Ema cried out to alert Custódio, who was outside on that luminous summer morning—"Custódio, come here!" And he came at once, and both of them stood examining the parcel from a distance, as if it contained a bomb, and she handed him a pair of kitchen scissors and he cut the string, which was so thick it looked like rope, and inside, rolled up and tied with another piece of string, was Walter's blanket. Maria Ema studied the surface of the object for a long time through her reading glasses, shocked by the contents of the package. She didn't know what to think, but felt disgusted enough to exclaim— "Can you believe it? It hardly seems possible that ten months after disappearing for good, he still comes back to offend us all, sending her that old blanket. He sends her that wretched blanket and upsets her all over again. He never had any shame. He comes back to trouble her even after he's dead." Custódio still has the kitchen scissors in his hand. "Well, be that as it may, it's her parcel"—said Custódio. "We shouldn't even have opened it, the package was addressed to her." And as she, at that moment, was standing before them, Custódio put down the scissors and handed her the parcel. Ten months had passed.

Ten months before, Adelina's voice had come clearly across from Vancouver—Not a house, not a car, not a dollar, not a suit, nothing. Walter had left absolutely nothing. He hadn't changed. She should have added—"Do you know, Pa, he didn't leave a bean!"

98.

But Walter did leave something.

To show that his fate had not been entirely predictable and to contradict everything that had been said about him, ten months later, the parcel containing the blanket arrived, addressed to his daughter. Written on the brown paper was her name and his, and inside was the blanket folded into sixteen, a bundle of thick, clean cloth, barely marked by the tight string around it. On the outside, the letters had been written in an impressively large hand, but the person who had written it had reversed the name of the town and the name of the country, which was given as São Sebastião de Valmares. And that is where the complications must have begun, because, as far as anyone knows, no such country exists. And yet, the parcel didn't get lost.

The unusual number of franked stamps on the package, along with the orders and requests written elsewhere on it, must have impressed at least two civil servants in Equatorial Africa, in search of such an addressee in Casamansa, another in Mexico, and yet another in Morocco, and finally someone in the south of Spain, in Málaga, whence it was forwarded to São Sebastião de Valmares, with another franking mark and someone else's dated initials. The stamps must have made an impression on the vulnerable hearts of those civil servants, who, quite coincidentally, worked in harmony with each other over a period of months, each touched by the whole appearance of the package. The parcel didn't look like something to be sent through the mail, more like a piece of paper found in the pocket of a drowned man. In sloping letters, in the crude hand of an uneducated person or of someone in a great hurry, could be read—POR AVION. URGENT. VERY URGENT. PLEASE TREAT AS A MATTER OF THE GREATEST URGENCY. And on the back, a note, a quite extraordinary statement—THE CONTENTS ARE OF SENTIMENTAL VALUE ONLY. PLEASE BE SO GOOD AS TO RESPECT BOTH SENDER AND ADDRESSEE. Walter Dias' daughter had no idea that you could sprinkle a parcel with such explicit messages, she was unaware there could be such a high degree of cooperation between such different places, especially when some of the words were already eroded by stains and fingerprints. The fact is, however, that Walter's last piece of correspondence ended up repeating the fate of the person who sent it, and Walter's daughter recognizes in that what she can only describe as a miracle. She knows no other word for it and doubts such a thing will ever happen again in her life. That is the only word. For is that mixture of silence, burlesque, coincidence and surprise not worthy of the name "miracle"? That, at least, is what Dr. Dalila in the house of the fig trees would have said, if we could have discussed Walter's final missive together. But there was more.

Inside the package, tucked inside the blanket, was a card written in Walter's elegant, slightly shaky, forward-sloping hand, with one last sketch of a bird–*I leave to my niece, as sole inheritance, this soldier's blanket.* It was as if from inside the life of a man there had emerged one very stubborn part offering a childish declaration of innocence, as when a child holds out its palms to prove its innocence. The blanket, slightly worn but clean, as it had been when he removed it from a barracks in Évora in 1945, was Walter's outstretched hand. How can the daughter stop saying "Wait"? Everything becomes clear tonight as he again comes up the stairs, bringing with him and the blanket a parade of extraordinary images that reconstitute all the old films. From the trips in the car to the photo of him with his arms around her, to the forgotten revolver, which, all on its own, spread fear and brought strength, to the summer afternoon when he had wanted to carry her off in the buggy to some unknown destination, to the anger of that dawn bonfire, and to the anger of that second dawn on Calle Morgana, when he had yelled at her "Get out!," even the genuine night of rain, and all the other nights when she used to call him and he would come. Now she knows that once more he will take off his shoes and come up the stairs whenever she asks him to. He doesn't have to apologize for anything or regret anything, nor ask anyone's forgiveness. He never did have to. Walter can wander about this space in peace, until the end of life itself.

99.

Wait–his daughter had said when he was closing the door of Bar Los Pájaros, after he had asked her to pass on his regards. And he closed it slowly, and because there was a spyhole in the door, she had stayed there for some time, certain he was look-ing at her through the spyhole. She had only left when it was time once again for the bar to fill up, because it was Friday, the holy Friday of bars, and the door constantly opened and closed, but there was no sign of him. And she walked back to the Residencial Las Naciones where she had taken a room, and then took the long road out to the airport, a road still per-vaded by that smell of evil acts perpetrated, which made a field, that should have been fertile, a sea of butcheries. "Wait"—she said, as she had on the night of rain. It was October 1983. She wanted to tell him that, even if they never met again, he should never think that he owed her anything, as she'd said on the night of rain. Because, in that lifetime of images, Walter Dias had left his daughter an immense fortune. But that was both true and false, because at the time, the daughter wanted to dis-card what Walter had left her up until then. But that will not happen tonight, there in front of his soldier's blanket, in a room at the top of the Valmares house. To which he returns, like a light, until the end of life itself.

100.

As it happens, the daughter knows the different tools as well as any laborer. She knows the plows, the shafts, the poles, the weeding hoe, the potato hoe, the three-, five- and six-pronged forks, the narrow spades like tongues and the concave ones like two large hands joined together. All these objects have been hung along the walls so that their children, at some future date, can turn the house into a museum for tourists, each tool labeled in acrylic. But meanwhile, she doesn't need any labels. She knows the sickle, the rake, the goad, the lifting hook with its one blade like a tooth, the one with two openings, thin as knife blades. She knows the hoe with the compact blade that cuts vertically into the earth with swift chopping movements, smooth as glass. And she knows the one with the curved blade, the one used for sifting out stones, for getting in between them and setting them to one side, removing them from the furrow as you dig. But this morning, she needs the solid hoe, with its one blade. But in order to dig with this hoe, a man has to raise it above his head, lift it straight up, having first spat on both hands, then, taking a firm grip on the handle, drive it in hard, with a grunt, letting the blade dig deep into the earth. That is the tool she is going to choose. And an area of earth, there, between the trees which were fruit trees, but which will soon be providing shade in a garden. It is on this tissue of sand that she is going to bring down the blade of that hoe. She knows where everything is, where each one of the tools can be found. The person currently sleeping with her in her room finds it strange that Walter's daughter should be able to look for an agricultural tool in the dark and find it just by touch, without having to turn on the light. It's in the skin, in the genes, in the blind eye in the middle of the forehead that sees all that is horrible and beautiful, while the rest of the body rests or even switches off entirely. She carries the tool and the blanket outside. The person with her cannot touch either, this is her business. Her business alone. With ancient gestures, she makes a hole in the earth.—"Ah!" With every blow she cries out as if she were giving birth to a child. She places the folded blanket in the hole, pleased with herself and with Walter. Who is whose father? Who is our mother? Perhaps, at that moment, Walter Dias has become her son. She hears the wheels of his innumerable cars, some of them in the form of ships, and she feels exhilarated by their speed, then afraid he might run off the road, over the berm and kill himself, exactly as one feels about a son. It is dawn again. We're together again, enjoying the drive. Please, wait.

And then, out of the side door of the Valmares house come Custódio's footsteps, measured, regular, his shorter leg protected by a strange layer of feathers, like fine velvet; they approach along the path, across the dry grass, on behalf of himself and of Maria Ema too, for she was wakened by the sound of her daughter digging in the middle of the olive trees. His serene, watchful foot approaches, the vigilant foot of a man who was one half of another man. Custódio reaches her side, takes the hoe from her, and he himself pushes the earth back, smooths it over, and waits for her to say something. Then he says—"For heaven's sake, don't just stand there, it's much too early to be up, go back inside." That is what he says. And then he too goes in.

The translator would like to thank
Lídia Jorge, Maria Eugénia Penteado,
Martin Jenkins, and Ben Sherriff
for all their help and advice.